Hyannis Boat
and Other Stories

Books by W. D. Wetherell

Souvenirs

Vermont River

The Man Who Loved Levittown

Hyannis Boat and Other Stories

Hyannis Boat
and Other Stories

by W. D. Wetherell

LITTLE, BROWN AND COMPANY
BOSTON   TORONTO   LONDON

The author would like to thank the National
Endowment for the Arts for their support
during the completion of this work.

FIRST EDITION

Grateful acknowledgment is made to the following publications
in which some of these stories were first published: newspapers of
the Syndicated Fiction Project: "Remembering Mr. C."; *The
Kenyon Review:* "Hundred Year War"; *Confrontation:* "The
Mall: A History"; *Gambit:* "Antediluvian Man"; *Quarterly
West:* "Brooklyn Wept"; *Green Mountains Review:* "The Next
Sound You Hear"; *TriQuarterly,* a publication of Northwestern
University: "What Peter Saw."

Library of Congress Cataloging-in-Publication Data

Wetherell, W. D., 1948–
  Hyannis boat and other stories.

  I. Title.
PS3573.E9248H93   1989   813'.54   88–26726

10 9 8 7 6 5 4 3 2 1

Designed by Robert Lowe

HC

*Published simultaneously in Canada
by Little, Brown & Company (Canada) Limited*

PRINTED IN THE UNITED STATES OF AMERICA

For Christina

Contents

Hyannis Boat
and Other Stories

Hyannis Boat

Uncle Daniel became rich after the war, but not in spirit. And when I say rich, I mean in the inflated, mid-century way that only in this one particular time, in this one particular culture could ever have been thought of as normal. The split-level with four bedrooms and a pool, the beach house even larger, the new cars with their ceaseless carbonizations, the new appliances and complicated toys. And when I say poor in spirit, I refer to the meager rewards these things brought him — how his last years were spoiled by the kind of remorse a pirate king might feel on the day the booty turns to ashes in his hands.

Of the war itself, I only heard him tell one story, this in the softened, apologetic voice that was all his disappointment left him. He had graduated a year ahead of his class at Boston Latin and spent the bulk of 1945 waiting for the fighting to end or his eighteenth birthday, whichever should come first. In the meantime, with the shortage of men, he found a job as deckhand on the old *Sconset* ferrying passengers and foodstuffs between Nantucket and Cape Cod. It was back-breaking work, with endless hours loading bulky containers of freight, but at least it helped exhaust the patriotic energy that — between newsreels and bond drives and victory gardens — coursed through his veins in unadulterated adrenaline.

At times it was better than that. At times they would leave the island late and be caught mid-passage by darkness so there was no separation between the sea below and the sky above, and their wake would sparkle with phosphorescence like a furrow plowed through stars. Watching it, Daniel would imagine he was on a troopship bound for Guadalcanal, an LST bound for Normandy, the *Queen Elizabeth* bound for home — feel danger and safety surge in alternate thrills of pleasure down his spine. Two miles out from Nantucket, Captain Bowen would douse all the lights, heightening the effect even more. U-boats were about, at least off Chatham, and though they had never actually seen one, there were gasoline cans piled on the stern to be floated toward anything suspicious and set ablaze with a deer rifle Newcomb, the mate, had commandeered from a sporting goods store back in Bourne.

Real or not, the threat helped them through the tedium of the night. Before long, what few passengers they had would be wrapped in their overcoats asleep, and Daniel would be left alone with his imaginings, staring out across the rail toward the uneven darkening that was America fifteen miles off the bow. Chalke, the engineer, would bring him coffee at midnight. The hot taste of it against his shivering gave Daniel a happiness that went beyond anything he had ever known.

This was May, the last few moments of the European war.

Each of the crew felt the excitement of this, and all their actions had been subconsciously quickened. With no returning passengers to worry about, the cargo was loaded at Nantucket that evening in record time. Bowen — prudent, unhurried Bowen — steamed them backward from the pier before the cargo doors were even secured, narrowly avoiding collision with a barge. The hurry was wasted though. They caught the first wisps of fog off Brant Point, and by the time they left the breakwater, long marbled strands of it had become caught up in the radio mast like streamers of taffy.

Bowen pitched around in it for an hour, then — with darkness — shut down the engines and glided the *Sconset* to a stop. Certain fogs on that sound seemed to sharpen and particularize, coating everything with wetness like a moist lens, but this was the darker, more dangerous fog that swelled and distorted, until even a bobbing seagull, ten yards off the stern, loomed as large and threatening as a tanker.

Daniel was sent aft to keep watch. The sea was weed-slicked and still — still enough that he took a seat on the biggest, most precariously balanced of the gasoline cans, straddling it like a pony. For three hours he sat there, blowing on his hands to warm them, stomping his feet up and down, working his gum around to sweeten the coppery taste of the fog.

By the fourth hour he was cold — cold and mutinous. It was ridiculous posting him there. No trawler in its right mind would blunder about in a pea soup like that. Even if one approached, there was nothing he could do to stop them short of launching Newcomb's gasoline bombs. He teetered there in indecision for another half hour, then with a righteous disregard of all consequence, swung himself down and began groping his way along the oily deck toward the bridge.

Daniel, in telling this, would clear his throat here, attempting to find the proper register to convey what happened next. He had walked all the way to the bow, cut through the deserted passenger lounge, and was just beginning to climb the iron stairway to the upper deck, when from the oval swelling in the side where the Number Two lifeboat hung there came a voice. A voice, or rather a voicelike sound, so deep and so troubled his first impression was that the fog, pressed so thickly, had chosen that moment to groan.

"Away!"

It was startling enough, coming out of the dark like that, but at the same time there was something so impossible about the deepness that Daniel hurried past the word's echo with the same kind of heedless, swiping gesture he would have used to brush away spray. He ran up the stairs to the next deck, felt his way around some hawsers, then continued on toward the wedge of orange that leaked from the blacked-out bridge.

The *Sconset*'s bridge was as round and rusty as the turret off an old Civil War ironclad, and it took a determined shove to open the door. Inside, the only light came from the crimson of the binnacle, but compared to the fog it was like daybreak. Daniel blinked his eyes to adjust. Bowen's pipe, the baked smell of the heater — he was aware of these first. Softly, braced for a scolding, he felt his way to the corner by the chart table where he would be out of the way.

No one bothered noticing him. Bowen sat on a stool to the side of the wheel, his mouth arranged in the thin smile that was his habitual expression, his pipe underlining it, his lips working meditatively on the stem. To his left stood Medeiros, his hands on the wheel even though the ship was motionless, his chin jutting out between spokes like a grizzled figurehead's. Chalke stood toward the front by the window, dressed in overalls. Beside him, balancing nervously on the balls of his feet, Newcomb rubbed sloppy circles across the glass.

"It was right there, I tell you," he said, to no one in particular. "Right smack there off the starboard bow."

"You're dreaming," Bowen said pleasantly.

"Bullshit I'm dreaming. Pat saw it too, didn't you, Pat?"

"Sure I saw it," Chalke said, without conviction. He wiped a mustache of grease across his lip. "It was . . . uh. It was yellow and red." He glanced over his shoulder for support. "Right, Joe?"

Medeiros — who was oldest — snapped his head forward in a spitting motion. "Fucking Krauts," he mumbled.

The three of them stared toward the window and the holes Newcomb was making in the steam. Only Bowen seemed disinterested. He swiveled around to refill his pipe, caught sight of Daniel, and winked.

"Pretty chilly there on the stern, eh, Mr. Mathews? Deserting your post is a capital offense. Pull up a stool and make yourself at home."

That was Bowen's way — not to miss anything, but to scold only gently — and Daniel idolized him as a result. He was the senior captain on the sound, retired when war broke out, then pressed back into service with a schedule that could kill a younger man. He was showing the strain of it now; despite the smile, there was a stiff, formal weariness about him, as if he were waiting for history to snap his picture so he could relax.

"The mate here's been seeing Martians," he said, without malice. "You might slide yourself forward and take a look. Fog like this needs young eyes to penetrate. You see anything with a green complexion, you let Mr. Newcomb know."

Newcomb spun around in Bowen's direction, saw Daniel, and vented his fury on him instead.

"Your post is at the stern, Mathews! Who the hell gave you permission to come forward?"

Newcomb was only two years older than Daniel and hard toward him for that reason. He was a big man, quick and alert — handsome if you didn't count the withered arm that made him 4F. His personality was a mix of boyish exuberance and low cunning, and he was spoken of among the ferry men as an up and coming young man.

"You get on back there now," he said. "You leave again, I'll —"

He was cut off by Chalke's yell. "There it is! There it is! Three points off the starboard bow!"

His voice was so certain that the five of them, even Bowen, rushed to the window this time. Daniel used his sleeve to clear off a space. At first, all he could see was the same impenetrable fog they had been wrapped in since stopping, but toward the top the droplets were less opaque, more scrimlike, and above that was a slight blackening that might possibly with some imagination be taken as sky.

"There's nothing," Bowen said.

Newcomb tapped the glass with his fist. "There to the right. Up high off the horizon. It must be every thirty seconds. . . .   Twenty-seven . . . twenty-eight . . . twenty-nine . . ."

Daniel, staring toward the blackness, saw it quiver — saw it spiral upward in a shaft of something red, then stop, widen, and drop.

"Over to port!" Chalke yelled. "Orange this time. No, cherry. Cherry-colored and higher."

"There's a silver one back the other way!" Newcomb said. "Silver and red and blue!"

Bowen, who had taken the binoculars out, focused them in the direction Newcomb pointed. "Flares," he said, after a time.

Medeiros nodded. "Ship in distress. U-boats. . . . Fucking Krauts."

"Flares my ass!" Newcomb shouted. He bobbed his head up and down and made little boxing motions with his fists. "Flares over dry land? Flares my ass! Flares don't blossom out like that. Flares aren't in colors. Those are fireworks!"

"In the middle of May?" Chalke said.

"Middle of May my ass! They're celebrating. The Cape is celebrating. You know what they're celebrating? You know what they're hot goddam fucking celebrating? The war is over! The war is fucking over!"

The moment he said it the fog, with its own sense of drama, parted enough to admit a narrow opening off the bow. Through it, a packet of light climbed into the sky and burst apart in a red, white, and blue cloud. A moment later the fog closed back again, but not until — very faint, more as a tapping sensation on the chest than anything aural — came the faintest, vaguest of booms.

"Sweet God in heaven," Bowen said. He put the binoculars down and wiped his eyes, suddenly very old. "You're right, Mr. Newcomb, and I apologize. Those are fireworks and there can be only one reason for them. The war is over."

With that they grew very solemn. Newcomb went around pumping all their hands, then Bowen did the same more formally, then Chalke with an embarrassed swiping, then Medeiros with cranky jerks. They went back to the window after that. Chalke fiddled with the radio but nothing came in.

"Well, what are we waiting for?" Newcomb said, when the silence grew noticeable.

"Waiting?" Bowen said.

"The war is over. The Cape is celebrating. Let's go."

"In this fog? We'd run straight up on a rock — a rock or a trawler."

Newcomb threw his arms apart and appealed in agony to the ceiling. "Then we'll miss it!"

"Now calm down, Mr. Newcomb. Let's not get hasty."

"Hasty!"

"What we need are those stronger glasses. Daniel? You know that locker back in the stern under the collapsibles? Go back and fetch it. . . . And Daniel?"

"Yes, sir?"

"Mind your footing. The last thing we need is an unconscious deckhand."

Daniel nodded, pressed his shoulder against the door to open it, then pressed it shut again on the angry, muffled sound of Newcomb's voice.

It didn't take long to retrace his steps. Despite Bowen's caution, he ran as fast as he could, hurdling the hawsers, swinging around a stanchion, all but flying down the stairway in sheer exhilaration. The war was over! The war was over and it was the happiest moment in his life and the happiest moment in America's life and the happiest moment in history and it was so happy that happiness swarmed in front of him like the fog and he couldn't think.

He was down to the main deck, ducking to get beneath the lifeboat davits, when out of the corner of his eye he noticed a blurred, back and forth motion slightly higher than the rail. At the same time, or even a split second sooner, he remembered the strange sound he had heard there on his way to the bridge. Between them, the blur and the remembering seemed to squeeze out a word the same way the fog had earlier, only this time in a whisper that was so throaty and urgent it stopped him dead in his tracks.

"Away!"

Daniel looked toward the lifeboat, saw nothing, and was just about to continue on when another, more distinct motion made him cross to the railing where he could stare up toward the L-shaped mount. There perched on the metal lip of it, his hands braced against the lifeboat's side, was a man dressed in a white linen suit.

Daniel's reaction came in three parts, the second and third following so hard upon the first it was impossible to separate them. It was a ghost he was looking at, a ghost materializing out of the mist, but not a ghost, a German saboteur bent on revenge, only not a saboteur but a stowaway — a stowaway who was athletic and nimble and deranged.

Was he dreaming? He craned back his head. There was a man there, only now he had left the relative security of the mount and was kneeling on the taut canvas of the lifeboat's cover, pulling frantically at the snaps. He seemed infuriated at their stubbornness; he ripped off his jacket, flung it sideways like a matador, then turned and went back at the snaps with redoubled fury.

"Away!" he said. "Away! Away!"

Daniel watched him with his mouth open, his fright changing very rapidly into guilt. Passengers were his responsibility, from the moment they boarded to the moment they disembarked, and to admit one had slipped aboard without paying would mean a tongue-lashing from Newcomb, possibly even firing. So there was no use being polite about it. He cleared his throat self-importantly, reached up, and rapped his fist against the lifeboat's keel.

"Hey you! Get down off there!"

"Away!"

"You heard me. Down from there!"

"Away!"

"Get down!"

Slowly, reluctantly, the man balanced his way along the boat's side and let himself down onto the locker where the lifejackets were stored. It still wasn't all the way to the deck, but it was flatter there and he was less likely to fall overboard.

"That's better," Daniel said. "Lifeboats are off-limits to passengers except during drills. Now where's your ticket? You're supposed to hand it in when you board. Come down here where I can make you out."

The man took a cautious step forward, but seemed unwilling to move beyond reaching distance of the boat. The white of its lapstrake, backing him, caught what soft light his face managed to cast, catching him up in his own milky radiance. He was thirty at most — blond and oval-faced, handsome in a leathery way, but with cheeks that seemed deflated and eye sockets that looked gouged. The rest of him looked drawn as well. His neck where his tie was loosened, his arms where his sleeves were rolled back. As strong as they were, they were lined with veins and prominent tendons, making it seem as if his body had been twisted together from cords.

"Here, all the way," Daniel said, softening his tone. He pointed toward the bridge. "It's not too late. I can sell you a one-way and nobody has to be the wiser."

The man was kneeling on the rail — he had started to lower a cautious leg to the deck — when behind him in the distance a new salvo of fireworks went shooting skyward, coloring the top of the fog in a hazy filigree of red and yellow.

The man's expression, wound so tight already, now seemed to snap past bearing. He leapt to his feet and hurled himself toward the lifeboat, beating the davits with the rolled mallets of his fists.

"Away!" he shouted. "Away, away, away!"

Each new blaze of light terrified him more than the last — he jerked crazily about, as if the explosions weren't on the horizon but in his heart. Daniel, for his part, had a new rush of panic, but only because he suddenly realized who the man must be.

The military squareness of his shoulders, his tanned face that displayed so much suffering, the horror the flaring caused. He was obviously a discharged soldier suffering shell shock — someone whose nerves had been shattered by artillery fire in Italy or France. A soldier, not a sailor. A sailor would have known where the winch was that lowered the lifeboat. He was still fumbling with the davits, all but biting them in frustration, sobbing out the same word again and again.

"Away! Away! Away!"

I must humor him, Daniel decided. I must speak plainly and simply like a friend.

"Don't be frightened. It's all right now. Those are fireworks, that's all. The Cape's celebrating. The war is over — at least we think so. Word must have come in tonight on the news."

"Away!"

"Away where? We're not in a battle or anything. Uh, were you in tanks? The Captain's son is in tanks. I think tanks must be . . . well, demanding. Pretty goddam demanding. It worries him but he never lets on."

"Away!"

"You must be happy it's over."

"Away!"

Daniel started to say something, then shrugged. Short of wrestling with him, there was nothing he could do alone. He waited to make sure the man had his balance, then turned and hurried toward the bridge for help.

They had taken down the blackout curtains since he left; the chart light and overhead were both fully on. Bowen and Medeiros stood near the wheel, saying nothing. Newcomb and Chalke stood to starboard as far from them as possible. From the way they glared at each other, it was obvious the silence had lasted a long time.

They waited while Daniel brushed the damp off his jacket. He had finished — he was trying to find the right words to explain — when Newcomb made a snorting sound and stepped forward.

"Okay, there it is. Two for, two against. Mathews, your vote decides. . . . Joe and the Captain say we molder in the fog where we are. Pat and I say we stop pussyfooting around and get under way and be part of the greatest celebration the Cape's ever known. . . . Which one for you?"

The four men looked at him — it was as if each had reached over and grabbed a separate limb. Go, with caution, Daniel decided to say, but before he could, Bowen leaned over and rapped his pipe against the wheel.

"You've been watching too many newsreels, Mr. Newcomb," he said quietly. "This isn't a democracy, not while I'm in charge. The kid doesn't vote. We wait out this fog if it takes a week."

Newcomb clutched his middle as if he'd been drilled. "Then we'll be late!"

"Late for what?" Bowen said.

"Late for everything! Late for the broads! Late for the

booze! What's waiting there? I don't know. Let's get this tub moving and find out. All it's been for four lousy years is the war this and the war that and now it's the war nothing and every poor lonely slob in the world is celebrating except us."

Bowen shook his head. "There's still Japan."

"Japan," Medeiros mumbled. He ground his dentures together, rearranging them from right to left. "Fucking Nips."

"Fuck Japan!" Newcomb yelled. "That's the other half of the world for crissake! In my half, the war's over. . . . Look," he said, changing tacks, "it doesn't have to be all that dangerous. The fireworks are enough to give us a horizon. We'll keep her down to six knots, keep blasting the hooter, stop the moment we see anything. In an hour we'll be docked at Hyannis cranking up my Ford ready to trot. . . . Right, Pat?"

Chalke, who was twirling pliers around on his finger, caught them and shrugged. "It's wiped the slate clean. The war, I mean. It's wiped the slate clean for the start of a new dawn." He looked up and shrugged again. "I read it in the *Post*."

Ahead of him and quite plainly, a firework climbed above the fog. It's explosion, coming clearer now, rattled around the bridge like something trapped.

"You know what this night is going to be known as?" Newcomb said, staring straight at Bowen. "It's going to be known as Victory Night 1945 — the night old Isaac Bowen lost his nerve."

Bowen, back on his stool now, didn't seem to hear. When he spoke it was very softly, to the glass.

"You don't push out here, understand? You poke and you probe and gain a few yards, but you never push, never force yourself. I can wait forever, that's my strength. That was the strength of the men that taught me, that was the strength of the men that taught them. That was all our strength."

"But not mine," Newcomb said. He crossed to the wheel. "I'll steer. Mathews, you go down to the bow and mount a lookout. The minute you see anything, scream."

"We're waiting it out," Bowen said, but the vigor was gone from his voice. "Ken, I'll tell you this man to man. It's going to sit bad with the authority your talking like this. It's going to mean a black mark when it comes to your future."

"My future?" Newcomb threw his arm toward the window. "There's my future! There with those lights. You think I'd stay in this lousy dead-end job one second after getting ashore? Fart around playing sailor for a lousy fifty a week? The minute my feet hit that dock I'm gone. . . . And why the hell are you standing there playing with yourself, Mathews? You heard me. Move!"

Daniel took a step toward the door, checked himself, and looked toward Bowen for confirmation. All during the argument he had found himself sharing Newcomb's impatience, but at the same time wanting the Captain to stand firm. Now, facing him, he saw something he had been too stupid to notice before — that Bowen himself shared their impatience; that his haste leaving Nantucket hadn't been a fluke; that his eyes, wherever else they went, kept swinging back to the distant glowing.

"You go down there like the mate says, Mr. Mathews," he said. "Mr. Chalke, you go down to the engine room and get up steam. If the fog breaks enough to see our bow lights, we'll get under way." He glanced over at Newcomb. "But only then, understand? Until it does, we're staying put."

Across the binnacle, Newcomb smiled. "Suit yourself,

Captain," he said, stroking his arm. "Hey, I'm in no hurry. No hurry at all."

Chalke grabbed his pliers off the transom and shot out the door like an unwound spring. Daniel, though, still hesitated.

"Well, what is it, Mr. Mathews?" Bowen said. "Are you going or not?"

"There's a man."

"What man?" Newcomb demanded.

"A man . . . I have to see a man. There in Hyannis, I mean."

Bowen rolled his eyes toward the ceiling in a Mother of God expression. "Now don't you start in on me too, Daniel. Get on forward like the mate says."

"Yes, sir."

Again, for the second time that night, Daniel pushed his way back out into the dark. It was harder this time. It was as if the fireworks had tilted the ship toward land, so that he had to fight gravity to make any way. He felt burdened besides — burdened with the weight of a secret and a lie. Between his worry over this, the clatter of his shoes, and the muffle of the fog, he didn't hear anything until he actually reached Number Two, and even then the sound seemed weaker than before, more wistful and slurred.

"Away . . . away . . . away . . ."

The man was still there, only now he knelt partially obscured in the center of the lifeboat, where he had managed to find the winch. He ran his hands over its mechanism quickly and carefully, probing like a safecracker, but without success. As simple as the winch was, there was a sleeve across the safety catch that kept the lifeboat from dropping. It took a certain familiarity to work it, and there was no risk of him doing it alone.

Daniel coughed to announce his presence, then spoke very

quietly, in the tone someone might use in coaxing a cat down out of a tree.

"I just talked to the Captain. He says you can ride free the rest of the crossing. In honor of the war being over, that is."

"Away."

"You could sit in the lounge if you wanted. It's a lot warmer in there. There's a cigarette machine. I could brew up some coffee."

"Away."

"There's a boat back to Nantucket at eight tomorrow morning. We could put you on that. That'll get you away, all right. I mean, you are from Nantucket. Your loved ones and so on?"

"Away!"

Each time he said it, a little more of his face edged past the planking, until all of it was exposed but the mouth. If anything, it showed even more desperation than before. Sweat made his forehead look feverish; grease underlined the skeletal ridges of his cheeks. When it became obvious the winch wouldn't release, he threw himself sideways across the middle seat, then sideways back the other way, trying to shake the boat loose by sheer force.

"Away!" he yelled, louder this time. "Away!"

Five minutes, ten minutes — Daniel wasn't sure how long the swaying lasted. As abruptly as he'd begun, the man left off and went back to running his hands along the winch.

"Wow," Daniel said, forcing a laugh. "You rock pretty good there. I bet this would be a good time for a rest. Besides, I see your suit is torn and —"

"Away!"

"I mean . . . Well, put it this way. I've been trying to help you for quite a while now. I've risked my job, stood out

here in the cold, even lied for you. Don't you think it's time
you compromised a little?" He put his hand up. "No, that's
okay. I know what you're going to say. But just trust me.
Here, put your feet on the davit over here and I'll give you
a boost down."

"Away!"

Daniel brought his hands back as if burned. "Okay! That's
it! I give up. You want to stay up there, that's fine by me.
Sorry. Stay up there all night for all I care. I'm going to
leave you all by your lonesome. . . . I'm going now. I won't
be able to help you down anymore. . . . I'm going to the
bow. See? I'm going up to the bow where I was supposed to
be all along. Here I go then. Here's my first step . . ."

The man showed no sign of noticing. Daniel took a second
step, scuffing his shoes, but the man still didn't notice and,
by the time Daniel had backed all the way to the stairway,
he was pawing as single-mindedly as ever at the winch.

"Have it your way then!" Daniel yelled.

He continued on toward the bow, his face burning the way
it did under one of Newcomb's tongue-lashings. There was
a tangle of cable there and he kicked it angrily apart,
then — his fury slackening — stepped up onto the anchor
flukes so he could look out toward the fog. It was worse than
before — thicker, blacker, with a faster roll off the water.
Still, there was a top to it, and by craning back his head —
craning it far back the way he did at the movies when he sat
too close — he could make out the horizon above the Cape.

The celebration there was reaching its climax. There were
fireworks far to the west over New Bedford, fireworks dead
ahead over Hyannis, fireworks over Brewster and Falmouth
and Orleans. They shot into the air in bundled columns of
sparks, disappeared momentarily, then burst apart in outspreading umbrellas that slowly merged, until the coast was

covered with a dome of shimmering, parti-colored flakes. And what was odd, though the sound traveled across the water like the pops of opened champagne, the light, as it lingered, seemed to become more garish and confused, so that at the last moments — as the final jubilant barrages were flung into the sky all at once — the horizon took on the molten, churning ugliness of overheated metal the instant before it cools into slag.

Daniel watched it wash out into the fog, trying to make sense of it all. It wasn't simple — nowhere near as simple as he had thought. His guilt over leaving the man alone, his guilt over letting him slip aboard in the first place, the danger of his falling overboard and drowning. Daniel's responsibility was too great, and after another minute of helpless staring, he clapped his hands together in decision and started back toward the lifeboat.

"Away?" he said, out loud. "I'll show him away, all right."

He was halfway there, plotting out exactly where on the body he would tackle the man in order to haul him down, when there was a scraping noise up above him to port — a scraping, then a hissing. He looked and was just in time to see a flare shoot up from the bridge and burst apart in white sparklers, illuminating the entire ship. Immediately, there was a second, third, and fourth, the booms and the flashing coming so hard upon each other that he was deafened and blinded all at once. There were whistles, blasts of the fog-horn, smoke pouring from the stacks. Beneath his feet, the deck plates, already shaking, sagged, stiffened, and throbbed.

What happened next came fast in a blur. The ship shot forward with a lurch hard enough to throw him against the rail. By the time he picked himself up again they were moving through the fog at what for the *Sconset* was breakneck speed. Up near the bridge, silhouetted in its light, Newcomb launched flare after flare toward the horizon, whooping and yelling at the top of his lungs. Below him, the smoke went from vertical to horizontal in one abrupt tilting, enveloping his legs. Closer, to starboard, the sea slid past like a slide down which they were racing; the fog, so flat until now, streamed backward with the smoke, stinging Daniel's eyes until they filled with tears.

The suddenness of it was enough to knock a steady man overboard, let alone a shaky one, and Daniel forced himself aft against the ship's momentum, expecting the worst. Back to him, he told himself, beating at the fog to clear his eyes. Back to him! Back to him! Back to him!

When he reached the lifeboat the man was where he had left him by the winch, only now he was holding it in close to his cheek, hanging from it, his shoulders slumped in exhaustion, the cords of his muscles extended and slack.

"Away," he mumbled, barely managing the sound.

He didn't see Daniel approach. It would have been no trick at all to grab him by his arms and cradle him like a baby to the deck. Daniel was bracing himself against the rail to do just that when the man's head lolled to the side and his eyes flickered open and he stared at Daniel as if seeing him for the first time.

"Away," he murmured. "Away."

Daniel was close enough now that he could see the reddish stubble of the man's beard, feel the soft touch of his breath against his cheek. "Away," he pleaded, but only in a whisper, and Daniel had to lean even closer and cup his hands over his ears to make the word out.

"Away?" Daniel said gently. "Away where?"

"Away," the man whispered.

"Far away?"

"Away!"

"Away?"

"Away!"

"Away where, goddammit!"

"Away!"

Above them the flares were exploding and the foghorn was booming and the whistle was screaming and their voices grew louder to surmount all the din until they were both yelling the word as loud as they could, their faces touching, their hands meeting on the winch. They were yelling and the man was pounding his head on the winch in agony and Daniel was sobbing and everything became mixed with the night and the flashing and the rushing until it was too much for him and Daniel slid the man's hand down the winch to the sleeve and pushed with him until the safety snapped free.

With a tearing sound and a furious kicking, the winch started to unwind.

It didn't take long. In a second the lifeboat had dropped below the rail, and a second after that came a splintering sound as it careened off the side and slapped against the water twenty feet below. Daniel, certain the man had been spilled out, grabbed hold of the empty davit and swung himself onto the locker so he could see down. Though the concussion had knocked him back off the seat, the man was still aboard — he was scrambling to right himself, grabbing furiously for the oars. There was a critical moment as the lines came taut — the boat hydroplaned wildly, nearly capsizing — but the man somehow managed to balance his way forward to unfasten the last hook.

As the boat dropped loose, the billow of the side took it from view and Daniel had to rush to the stern to pick it up again. By the time he did, the lifeboat was already well back of them, pitching in the heavy V of the wake. The man, shirtless now, had the oars out and was rowing steadily toward the open sea, his back dipping and straightening with each new stroke.

"Away!" he yelled, the distance emphasizing the force of his voice, so that it rang across the water with the pealing, tolling defiance of a bell. "Away! Away!"

He pulled the boat through the froth of black weed and creamy phosphorescence the propellors churned up, until the gap between them was twenty yards, then forty yards, and then the boat was into the fog, the bow disappearing first, then the man's shoulders, then the man's head, then the tapered pentagon of the lifeboat's stern, and then there was nothing left in the story but Daniel as a young man watching it and Daniel as an old man telling it and the senselessness of the word's repetition and the final diminishing echo drawing the circle fully shut.

"Away. Away, away, away, away . . . away, away . . . away . . . away."

Away.

Remembering Mr. C.

T HE DRIVER turned the music up when they crossed into
Vermont. Even worse, he began steering to the beat. Mrs.
Tonelli, leader of the Holy Rosary ladies, balanced her way
to the front of the bus to ask him to be more careful. Before
she could get there, he stepped on the gas, sending her
flying. Mrs. Bouchard, leader of the Sacred Heart group,
tried next. She was almost up to him — they could see her
hand fluttering above his shoulder as she summoned up the
nerve — when he snapped his fingers, dipped his head,
swerved across two lanes at once. "Oh, yeah!" he laughed,
beeping the horn. Mrs. Bouchard tumbled sideways into
Sister Tremblay's lap.

Three rows farther back, Mrs. LeBlanc bowed her head in
prayer. "A bad man," she whispered. "A very bad man."

Mrs. Cormier, her seat-mate, was a little frightened by
the way she said it. Most people she knew prayed softly,
even apologetically, but Mrs. LeBlanc prayed in incanta-

tions, curses, and threats. Finishing, she brought her head back up, unfolded her hands, took out a hanky, and began to wipe off each finger in turn.

"The foliage is his fault, too," she said. She said it loud enough that the Sacred Heart people could hear. There were numerous nods.

The leaves were gray and drab-looking back in Worcester, but everyone had high hopes for "the autumnal pageant of the hills" as described in Sister Tremblay's brochure. And of these hopes, none soared higher than Mrs. Cormier's. Vermont had always occupied a special place in her heart, even though she had never been there. Vermont, the thought of it, was like one of the room fresheners she hung on the doorway to ward off the cooking smells of the Pakistani family next door — a cool, green, refillable relief. When the bus passed the Leaving Massachusetts sign, she had sat back rigid in her seat, braced for . . . Well, she didn't know really. Something anyway. Something besides Mrs. LeBlanc blowing her nose.

"There's a gold one," Mrs. Cormier said timidly.

Mrs. LeBlanc squinted. "A beer can, dear. The driver has deliberately taken us down the least leafy road."

Mrs. Cormier had to admit that Mrs. LeBlanc was right. The leaves were brown — a soft brown. Back in Worcester, she was afraid to walk under the trees in October because the leaves were spiky and she couldn't help worrying that they would drop from the branches and pierce her skull. Vermont leaves looked as though they would drop as gently as silk scarves. Even their color, dull as it was, attracted her. It reminded her of something, other brown leaves she had seen once before. She couldn't pin down where or when, but for the time being it was enough just to be vaguely reminded.

"At least we have the Presidential home yet," she said, hoping to brighten things up.

Mrs. LeBlanc smiled. "A good man," she said. "A good, kind man."

"Yes?" Mrs. Cormier said, hoping to learn more.

"I think they intended this armrest for the convenience of the person sitting in my seat, dear. Thank you. Now."

"The President?"

"His friends called him Herbie. A good, kind, clean man."

The two of them settled back in their seats, dwelling in satisfaction on the image of his cleanness. The bus had left the highway now. They were bouncing along a steep road through a valley shaggy with trees. There weren't any billboards anymore, hardly even signs. Ahead of them was a white church steeple backed by hills. The driver swung left, skidded across a wet spot on the pavement, then slammed on the brakes, bringing them to a stop beside a post office that was partly a house. To the side of it was a green historical marker with raised gold letters.

The driver picked up his microphone. "Calvin Coolidge homestead," he drawled. "Hour and a half. You're not back here on time, walk home." He jerked his thumb out and laughed. None of the ladies moved. "Get your white asses out there!" he yelled. Startled, Sister Tremblay waved the Holy Rosary group toward the door. Mrs. Cormier, as she edged past the driver's seat, kept her hand wrapped around the nail file in her purse.

Mrs. LeBlanc went down the steps backward on account of her hip. Mrs. Cormier steadied her, then together they joined the people walking along the road toward the homestead's entrance.

"Breathe in, dear," Mrs. LeBlanc said. She did herself,

sucking air through her lips like soda, then munching it on the back of her teeth like gum.

Mrs. Cormier tried a tiny sip. She would have tried more, but something was bothering her. "I thought you said this was Herbert Hoover's home," she said.

"Why on earth would I say that?" Mrs. LeBlanc replied angrily. "Coolidge, of course. I voted for him two different times. His wife was such a handsome woman. And over there is his house."

She pointed to the left. There beneath a spruce tree was a modest white-framed home with a barn. The Sacred Heart ladies were already lined up for tickets to go in. The Holy Rosary group, being on the whole older and slower, straggled along in pairs. A few of them headed up the hill toward another barn, this one with a big sign on the side: PLYMOUTH CHEESE CORPORATION JOHN COOLIDGE PRESIDENT. The ones with walkers went downhill toward a stone building that served as a museum.

"Do you see postcards anywhere?" Mrs. LeBlanc asked, with rare uncertainty. "Or should we start with some cheese? My Edgar always had such an interest in the Swiss varieties."

Mrs. Cormier didn't answer. She was marveling at how quiet and neat it all was. The trees shading the old weathered benches, the immaculate white paint of the buildings, the silence that even the idling bus engines couldn't dent — it was as if the entire village were tucked inside a transparent Tupperware bowl.

Mrs. LeBlanc tugged her arm. "I said, shall we try the home first?"

"If you'd like."

"Are they charging admission? Are they charging admission, dear? If they are, I'd rather forgo."

"It can't be very much."

Even the slightest challenge made Mrs. LeBlanc's face go red. "It's a rip-off, dear, but you go ahead if you want." She turned her back on the home and peered the other way, looking for an alternate destination.

It didn't take her long to find one. With a quickness surprising in someone her size, she hurried across the grass toward the simple white church they had seen from the bus. By the time Mrs. Cormier caught up with her, she was inside kneeling by the altar. Because of her hip, she couldn't kneel the ordinary way, but got down on all fours like one of those Iranians they were always having on TV. Hearing the tap of Mrs. Cormier's support shoes, she crawled to her left to make room, but Mrs. Cormier continued past her and set herself down in the first row of pews.

"And for the *unfaithful*," Mrs. LeBlanc prayed, "we ask thy forgiveness."

As tranquil as the village was, the church was even more tranquil. It was as if the kernel of peacefulness were located right there in the center of the pews where the light from the windows converged. Mrs. Cormier went over and sat so that the beams crisscrossed her head.

It was a simple enough church. There were no confessionals or stations of the cross or any of the clutter she found so distracting at Holy Rosary. The only decorations were stained-glass windows with sheep. She could see through the nearest one to the top of a small tree. It waved back and forth in the breeze, the leaves tugging to be gone. Pretty, she decided, and then she remembered what the leaves reminded her of: the tree outside the rooming house in Lowell where she had lived as a bride — the tree Omer had planted by hand. She couldn't remember what kind of tree it was, not exactly, but something told her it might have been a peach. Not a peach peach, but a brown peach, the kind that got left in the bottom of the bin after the fresh ones were sold. She remembered Omer coming home with the baby tree wrapped in burlap beneath his arm, remembered the hours he spent trying to coax fruit from its thin limbs, the water he sprinkled it with, the tender way he patted the dirt, and then like magic the tree was grown up and Omer was gone and the bark went scabby so she had to have the landlord chop it down.

"And her, too, Lord! Her, too!"

Mrs. LeBlanc was praying even louder now that the others were starting to come in. She flailed her rosary beads against the bare wood of the altar, emphasizing each word. Not to be outdone, three of the Sacred Heart ladies knelt down in the center aisle and began chanting in unison, until the little church throbbed so much it hurt Mrs. Cormier's ears. With a little nod toward the naked crucifix, she hurried outside.

This time she inhaled a good helping of air. It was cooler now, even fresher. The wind blew leaves across the grass, gold ones that swept past her into a big pile. For a moment, she was tempted to wade right through them, but she was afraid someone would see her and think she was silly.

The line at the home was still fairly long, so she decided to visit the museum first. It was in a neat-looking stone building across from the parking lot. A woman dressed like a Pilgrim handed her a brochure as she walked in. There were lots of pictures on the walls, most of them of President Coolidge. There was President Coolidge shaking hands with Babe Ruth, President Coolidge shaking hands with Jack Dempsey, President Coolidge shaking hands with Charles Lindbergh. The best picture showed President Coolidge in an Indian war bonnet. There were invitations, too, framed and mounted in little spotlights so you could read them without squinting. In a glass case was the necklace President Coolidge's wife had worn at the inauguration; beside it were President Coolidge's cuff links. Everything was very neat. Mrs. Cormier went around slowly so as not to miss anything.

When she was done, she went back to the picture of President Coolidge shaking hands with Charles Lindbergh. On the bottom was the date, 1927. What was funny wasn't the date, but the fact that she had been alive then. Not only alive, but twenty-two years old. She had been alive and breathing and living in Lowell, and yet all she could remember from those years was Omer and his peach tree — how he missed the New Brunswick woods he had grown up in, and how planting the tree was a relief from the factory noise that made him half deaf even though he wasn't thirty. She stared at the back of the picture where someone like him might have been. But no — 1927 refused to come into sharper focus. There was President Coolidge looking grim, and Charles Lindbergh looking embarrassed, and nothing else.

"May we ask your help?"

It was the Pilgrim lady. She stood there holding a cup trimmed in red, white, and blue felt. When Mrs. Cormier hesitated, she shook it so that the coins rattled inside.

"Certainly," Mrs. Cormier said. She put a nickel in the cup. When the lady still didn't go away, she added a dime. "Thank you," the lady said. Mrs. Cormier wasn't sure, but it sounded sarcastic.

She suddenly felt very much alone — it came over her just like a chill — so she hurried back to the bus to get her sweater. The driver was asleep with his ears plugged in and his feet on the dashboard. Rather than disturb him, she walked back toward the homestead, hugging herself in the cold. Now that it was lunchtime, most of the ladies were lined up in front of a tea shop to the right of the Presidential home. Mrs. Cormier decided to join them, but before she got there, a cramp in her right leg forced her to find a bench where she could rest.

It was a pretty enough spot. There were pine trees, but not so many that they hid the sun. Behind the trees was a little brook dancing through a meadow. It was easy to picture President Coolidge taking his Cabinet to fish there on summer vacations. A bit closer to the road was a stone well with a bucket resting on its edge. The well was neat and old-fashioned looking, and Mrs. Cormier decided that it was exactly the kind of thing Omer would have enjoyed. For a while this relaxed her — she felt the cramp dissolve into smaller knots — but then she realized that she had no particular reason for thinking Omer would have liked it at all. She didn't know what Omer would have liked. You live with a person for seven years, listen to his complaints, massage his back, offer to move to New Brunswick so he could be happy again, you'd think you'd remember something besides the sight of him stooped over a tiny peach tree spreading manure. But try as she might, that's all that would come.

"Hello, Mrs. Cormier!"

The sound floated on the breeze. There in the distance by the cheese factory stood Sister Tremblay, both hands pressed tight against her bonnet so it wouldn't blow off. Mrs. Cormier waved to show she was all right, even though she wasn't. She could still sense the overturned bowl covering the village, but it was less transparent now, murkier, locking her out. She got back up and walked around the homestead's perimeter, pretending to look for a rest room, while what she was really looking for was a gap in the bowl big enough to slip under.

She was on her third lap and beginning to get tired when the solution came to her. The President's house. Here she was moping around because she felt outside of things, and it was because she *was* outside. In the house, she would be *inside*. She hurried toward the entrance, one shoulder turned ahead of the other as if to break through the film that sealed it off.

The entrance was in the barn part of the house. She was reaching into her purse for the money when a hand shot out from the shadows along the wall and tightened on her wrist.

"There you are, dear. There you are."

Mrs. LeBlanc struggled to her feet. Apparently she had been sitting there all along. She didn't look like she was having a good time.

"I thought naturally you would wait for me while I made my devotions," she said. "I thought naturally we would have lunch together as planned."

Behind them, the ticket man snapped his ticket punch impatiently in the air.

"I was chilled," Mrs. Cormier said quickly. "I had a cramp."

"Well, never mind that now. All is forgiven. I do think however that we should be getting back to the bus. I was a bit carsick coming up. I would prefer a seat nearer the middle."

"I'm going to see the President's home."

"Oh. You are." Mrs. LeBlanc flexed her fingers back and forth as though she were getting ready to pray. "Then I'm afraid you'll have to sit alone. Alone, dear. By yourself near the driver."

And it was strange, but just then there was a little plastic

sound, and bang came down the Tupperware bowl so that
Mrs. LeBlanc was outside it, her threats bouncing off against
the sides. The plastic distorted her features so that her lips
became rubbery — not real rubber, but silly rubber, the kind
that flaps every which way.

"I'm going inside the President's home," Mrs. Cormier
said, raising her voice so Mrs. LeBlanc could hear.

"How much is it?" Mrs. LeBlanc was saying, though the
sound was very remote.

"A dollar!" Mrs. Cormier shouted, sticking up a finger.

She could see Mrs. LeBlanc wince. She could see her rubbery face flap every which way trying to come up with an
excuse.

"I'd love to accompany you, dear. But you see. Oh, dear.
You see, my Edgar was always such a staunch, a *very*
staunch Republican. He would be offended to think that I
would do something like this. He would . . ."

There was more, but Mrs. Cormier didn't wait. The ticket
man took her dollar and pushed her firmly toward the first
room. It was the pantry — there were shelves with all kinds
of tins. It wasn't that much bigger than the pantry they'd
had in the rooming house back in Lowell, but it was neater,
sunnier, with a lot more food. There were cheeses set out on
the cutting board, hams hanging from the rafters, jugs of
maple syrup, a crock of yellow cream. Everything seemed
ready for the Coolidges to walk in and start eating. A silk
cord was strung across the entrance so that no one could help
themselves to any of the food, but for Mrs. Cormier it was
enough just to look.

She went up the hall to the next room. It turned out to
be the kitchen. Again, everything was shined up spick-and-
span. Here she had gone into the house expecting it to be
old and musty like an attic, and instead everything smelled

like fresh-baked bread. At first, it troubled her — how could a home of dead people smell so much better than hers? — but the deeper into the house she went, the more convincing the smell became. It was exactly the way history *should* smell. Warm somehow. Uneaten. Edible.

She had finished with the kitchen and was heading up the hall when a guide lady came through with a group of schoolchildren. She was younger than the museum lady, and she was dressed more like Merle Oberon in *Wuthering Heights* than a Pilgrim. She stood in front of Mrs. Cormier to shelter her as the children rushed past.

"The room on the left was the President's study," she explained, in a voice soft as spring. "On his desk are his papers just as he left them when he died. Beside them you'll see a copy of his favorite railroad timetables. On the wall is a picture of his father, Judge Coolidge. The books on the shelves are from the President's student days at Amherst College in Amherst, Massachusetts."

Mrs. Cormier could see the schoolchildren taking it all in. "I was there, too," she was tempted to say. "In 1927 I was living in Lowell, Massachusetts, at 323 Thomas Avenue in a three-story rooming house on the third floor. I worked in a bakery rolling dough. My husband's hobby was planting trees."

She lingered by the study when the group moved on. What she liked best was the President's rolltop desk. It looked good as new. She could imagine President Coolidge laying his head on it when he worked late at night — actually picture him there, his round face creased in worry, his tired hands rubbing his eyes as he fought off sleep. It made her want to tiptoe. The spotless walls, the beautifully varnished floors. They made her want to tiptoe. When she tried to think of her own past she always wanted to run, but here was a refuge where she could remain forever, gliding softly from room to room, surrounded by the possessions of the man who was President when she was twenty-two. She had the feeling that if she stayed there long enough, even the peach tree would change somehow. It would still be a peach tree, but a good peach tree with actual peaches. She could picture them piled in a basket in the pantry, President Coolidge helping himself to a ripe one off the top.

Another group had come in behind her. Rather than being squeezed in the middle, she went up the hall to where the schoolchildren were leaning over a rope looking into another room. There was just enough space that she could see in, too. The guide was standing near a table covered with a simple lace doily. Resting on top was a black, leather-covered Bible.

"Can you all hear me?" the guide asked. It was difficult, because she had lowered her voice to a hush. "This is the room where the then Vice President Coolidge took the oath of office on August 3, 1923, when news reached Plymouth that President Harding was dead. Judge Coolidge administered the oath with his son's hand resting on the family Bible. In ordinary times, the room functioned as the parlor."

The children were quickly bored — they ran out the door, allowing Mrs. Cormier to move right up to the rope. It was the nicest room yet. There was a brown sofa and some high-backed chairs, a Victrola and lacy curtains. Next to the sofa was a wooden rocking chair. On a little stand just inside the rope, close enough to touch, was an embroidered cushion. "Bless this Home," it read. The letters were done in silk. The *B* was red and gold, the *H* was silver, and the little letters were emerald. Mrs. Cormier had never seen a cushion done so well. It was as if everything she liked about the

President's house had been sewn into a plump little bundle that smelled of lilac. The smell made her feel odd, almost dizzy, with the same chill that had shivered her in the museum.

She shook her head to clear it, but the feeling grew worse until it was almost like a convulsion. She was looking at the cushion, thinking how perfect it was, then like a flash she was remembering Omer, not with the peach tree this time but with his arms around her that last night before he went away to find work, and he was so handsome and so strong, and yet all she could remember of him had slipped into a bottomless white hole she was teetering over herself. It frightened her, made her want to grab hold of something to break her fall. She looked over her shoulder to find the guide. She was standing by the door watching the children, her back to the room. Mrs. Cormier reached into her purse for her nail file, reached over the rope for the cushion, turned it over and, with five quick strokes, sliced her initials across the bottom. By the time the guide turned around, the cushion was safely back in place on the stand.

Mrs. Cormier crossed herself and started for the door.

"Did you enjoy your visit?" the guide said pleasantly.

Mrs. Cormier nodded. "A good man. A home-loving man."

The bus was waiting for her by the post office. The driver was honking the horn, revving the engine. Pressed against the windows were twenty-five angry faces, the angriest of which was Mrs. LeBlanc's. Sister Tremblay stood leaning out the door urging her to run. But Mrs. Cormier was in no hurry now. She stopped to look back toward the President's home. There were eighteen — no, *nineteen* — on line for tickets. Men, women, boys, and girls. Later there would be more, eventually millions, and every one of them would file past her cushion in reverence.

"In reverence," Mrs. Cormier whispered. "Forever."

She watched them go in, then turned and walked toward the bus with the proud erectness of a woman whose place in history is secure.

Hundred Year War

Yಂou're not a cabbie," Hickson said, "not an authentic one-hundred-percent genuine made in the U.S.A. guaranteed-washable Yellow Peril cabbie until . . . You listening, gook face? . . . until you've killed your man."

His voice cut through static like a shark fin through water. As Ngo Quang careened up H Street toward New York Avenue, his hand left the steering wheel just long enough to turn the knob a delicate notch to the right. Hickson, though, was one thought ahead of him, and he only talked louder to make up the difference.

"You've killed your share anyway, right, No Dong? Hey hey, NQD, how many kids you killed today? But I'm talking civilians this time, pal. I'm talking bureaucratic pencil-pushing ass-kissing scum, the makers and shakers and fakers of downtown Washington, center of the universe circa 1988. You don't get a briefcase painted on that bumper before the day is out, you one ex-cabbie, dig? I call Immigration Service they heap mad send No Dong home on same leaky tub No Dong hijack to get here. . . . Hello, Yellow Peril Cab. No terrain too hostile, no cause too lost. Nineteenth Street? Right away, ma'am. We'll send our top driver over pronto. . . . Hear that, ND? Judging by the supercilious drawl, a senator's wife in the flesh. Big tippy. Twenty-five cents minimum. Move your urine-colored ass."

Hickson's voice was a shark's fin — a shark that had the steering wheel in between its infallible jaws — and it took a willful effort of disobedience for Ngo Quang to yank it free. He continued on New York until he came to Pennsylvania Avenue, made a left past the White House, then headed south toward Constitution. He could picture Hickson's anger when he found out — the way he would flail the dispatcher's desk with the corroded Bronze Star he used to crush flies; the way he would shimmy his wheelchair back and forth as if it were the metal itself that was having the contraction — but it was something he would have to risk. He reached over to flick on the Off Duty light, then returned his full attention to the task that occupied him most of the day. The chore — the difficult painstaking Hickson-defying chore — of not mutilating anyone with his cab.

It wasn't easy. In the dusty film of the November dusk, the dense snarl of jaywalkers, the explosion of traffic out from the garages, it wasn't easy to keep his bumper pure. Targets offered themselves at every corner. Young men with pasty faces and hard crusty eyes; women with the coiled tightness of so many Americans; tourists with their noses in maps. They would run for the safety of the traffic islands, bunch there rubbing shoulders like animals faced with slaughter, then jump out singly toward their extermination. When their eyes met his through the windshield they would open round in surprise — surprise and relief. Their arms

would spread apart as they turned to accept the collision —
their mouths would go slack in a signal that went beyond
words. "Take me," the look said. "Separate me from my
burden, sweep me away." There was something in the hope-
lessness of Washington's dusk, something in their tightness,
that made them all but jump beneath his wheels.

So he was very careful how he drove. As a boy in Hue,
the Buddhist monks had taught him to respect all forms of
life. Life was sacred, they said. Life was the be-all and end-
all, the eternal temple you have been appointed to guard.
And though Ngo Quang hated the monks for their sleek-
ness, the greedy way they hid saffron buns in the dark inner
folds of their robes, it was a lesson he remembered. On his
way home from school he would make elaborate detours to
avoid the armies of red ants that marched along in the deep
grooves of their ancestors. By tiptoeing, by hopping back
and forth, he could sometimes get all the way to his house
without killing a single ant. By swerving, by liberal use of
his horn, he could just barely manage to get all the way
down Seventeenth Street without killing a single pedestrian.

He accelerated into the stream of traffic on Constitution,
slowed to shrug it off, then made a screeching U-turn over
to the far curb near the monument. His usual spot was
crowded out between a deserted hot dog wagon and a Park
Service van, but by nudging both with his bumpers he was
able to make a space.

"Break time, huh, Ho Hong? Like a magnet, you can't
keep away from the place. I'll cover for you this time, but
you duck one more fare you're gone, savvy? I feed you to
Big Mac in little pieces. One good cabbie down the tubies.
You got better moves than anyone Yellow Peril's ever had,
good instincts, good directional sense, a gap-tooth smile the
old dames love, eyes that would do justice to Bambi. But

guts, I don't know. Guts you could be the best day-in day-out cabbie this town ever saw. The others didn't have guts. Pol Ping, Pol Pong. Here I gave them every chance, molded their immalleable Asiatic clay into something that could pass for decent, talked them around this town for two lousy years, gave them all my insight, and what happens? They tried to get smart. Tried to act like some Saigon hotshot rickshaw draggers who knew all the tricks. But you're different, ND. You listen and learn. You've got a brain of sorts, a smattering of a soul. So take five if you want it. Commune with ancestors, count tippy money, takey piss."

Even parked, the rush of traffic stayed with him, and in order to get away from it he got out and paced back and forth on the curb. There weren't many people around. A class and their teacher; some old people in funny hats; three or four Japanese. On the walkway leading in toward the monument, a young couple examined the name and address key the Park Service had mounted on a thick metal stand. The couple leafed through the pages slowly at first, as though it were the Bible, but by the end they were flipping the pages much faster, as if it were the phone book instead.

Ngo Quang took a cautious step toward the grass. Though the monument was still a good hundred meters away, it was the closest he had ever come. By rising up on tiptoe he was able to see heads dip and bob along the sunken lane at the monument's base. It made him think of the VC tunnels their American officers would order them to explode — how helplessly those assigned to do it trudged off into the dark. Even now, watching the tourists descend, he couldn't help but brace himself for an explosion, and he was surprised when the heads emerged on the far side, magnified and blackened by the setting sun.

"Ah, you'd like to go in, wouldn't you, Hoo Hung? Like to see dirty American memorial to dirty American war. Body-count time, right, ND? Bring in abacus to tally victims. Just try it, gook. A VC look-alike showing up in broad daylight? You'd be lucky to escape with your balls."

Harsh as it was, Hickson's voice was oddly reassuring, and for a moment Ngo Quang let it draw him back to the protection of the cab. Listening to him was like listening to shells fall in the distance on enemy emplacements, a chaos that was soothing.

"Yeah, that's the trouble with your basic gook cabbie. They're servile and inscrutable and devious and all those good Asiatic-type things, and here you got this monkey around your neck about this lousy monument. You'd think it was your monument, for Christ's sake. Like you'd done something to deserve our thanks. That's why half you boat people come in the first place, just to go sight-seeing. I bet they're printing up brochures in Hanoi right now. Visit Washington, see Vietnam Memorial, watch round-eye women throw bricks. Pol Ping, Pol Pong. They wouldn't listen to me, had to go in and see for themselves and look what happened. You think anyone cared they were ARVN good guys? A gook is a gook is a gook . . . Yellow Peril Cabs. Kennedy Center? Right away, sir. I'll send over our night-driving specialist at once. . . . Hear that, No Dong? A lobbyist and a fat one. Your last chance. The outcome of a congressional bribe is riding on this. I want you over there in five minutes, tops, and I'll pay double any ticket you get on the way."

Ngo Quang remained where he was. As wise and all-knowing as Hickson was, there were gaps his cynicism skimmed past. Though he was right about the temptation in Ngo Quang's heart, he was wrong about the motive. It wasn't to gloat that he wanted to visit the monument. It wasn't to satisfy a morbid curiosity or stir up anyone's resentment. It was much simpler than that. He wanted a name.

A specific name. The name of the American infantryman he had shot by accident near Tum Plang during the last days of Tet. At first, he had thought he might be able to locate it by simply looking through the mounted name and address key, but he understood now that this was impossible. Paper was too smooth and absorbant; he might run his hands over a thousand pages without finding the sympathetic vibration he sought. As a boy, the other children would bring him injured birds to nurse, respecting the skill and tenderness in his touch. As a soldier, he had volunteered to defuse booby traps and would shape his hands over their mechanisms as gently as he would stroke the smallest sparrow, rendering them harmless.

So there was knowing in his hands. The night he had fingered the soldier's dog tags trying to clean off the mud and blood so he could read his name he had felt a pulse so direct it made his arm go rigid, as if the last beat of the soldier's heart were flowing up the metal chain to his own. By that same pulse he would find him again. He would run his hands over the embossed names on the monument like a blind man reading braille, and when he got to the right one the current would be re-established — his fingers would stop.

With the name it was over. The pain, the fear and guilt. If he could find the soldier's name and read it to himself and say it out loud, then it wouldn't be a nightmare anymore, but something finished and real. Without a name the soldier was dying over and over again, raising himself up on his elbow in that same straining way, with no release in it, no completion. Named — his inscription located, his tragedy made particular — the soldier would finally settle into the cool oblivion of mud, freeing the two of them from the eternal torment of the wheel to which they were bound.

A magnet, Hickson had said. A force drawing him he could no longer resist.

He took another step to the left. There was ground mist where the grass began, and it immediately encircled his ankles, giving him the impression he had just stepped off land into a cloud. There were small hooded lights mounted along the walkway, marking the route. Farther ahead at the base of the monument, the lights flared up in a ring that was as white and glaring as phosphorus. On its fringe stood the last two visitors left: a woman and a taller man, the woman leaning against the man's shoulder like a crutch propping him up. They seemed reluctant to leave. The woman bent down and placed something at the base of the wall. The man — more stiffly — reached down and added something to whatever she had left.

Ngo Quang took three steps more, gaining confidence as the mist rose up his legs. To the left beyond the address key were some recently planted trees. They were saplings, their shadows as knobby and thin as a child's skeleton. Past them were some thicker shrubs that would hide him from anyone patrolling the path. Ten meters. Fifteen, perhaps. Where the shrubs ended was an open patch of grass with no cover of any kind. He would have to chance it there. Once to the monument itself he could press himself flat against the wall, hugging the shadows, but the open spot — all twenty meters of it — would have to be forced.

The thought of it made him sweat. To steady himself he counted to ten. He counted first in his own language, then in French, then in English. He was unbuttoning his shirt so that its whiteness wouldn't give him away, plotting out the course over which he would crawl, when there was a sudden blast of sound from the curb. Such was his concentration that it was a few minutes before he realized the sound was coming from his own cab.

It was the young couple he had seen turning through the address key. The man had an angry expression on his face; he was leaning in the front window pumping the horn. They were the kind of tourists Ngo Quang detested — the kind that visited the monument just to say they'd been there.

"Where the hell were you hiding?" the man said. "The Hilton and make it quick."

Ngo Quang dipped his head in a little bow and went over to the passenger door. As the couple waited, he reached in as if to sweep off the seat. Instead, he flicked down the lock. By the time the couple understood what it meant, he had locked the other three doors and was back in his own seat rolling up the window.

"No duty," he said, shaking his head. "No duty."

The man's face turned red — he banged his fist angrily against the roof. The noise, rattling the dashboard, was loud enough to carry across the mike.

"Up to your old tricks, huh, No Dong? No pity for the historically inept, no rememberee no ridee, let them find rickshaw. But poor business, ND. You haven't had a fare in three hours now. Here I am sticking up for you victimized left-in-the-lurch true-blue ARVN cabbies and this is how I get repaid? You're slipping, Soo Song. Going route of compatriotic Ping and Pong. I warn them about Big Mac, but Ping and Pong no listen, think I making Big Mac up. We go see pretty monument at night when no one around no one notice us. Big Mac not legend I tell them. Big Mac eat Yellow Peril cabbies for dessert."

At first, Ngo Quang listened the dreamy way he always did, responding more to the rhythm than the words, but at the last sentence he sat straight up and leaned forward with the same concentration he had brought to reconnoitering the terrain.

"Interested? You should be interested you lousy Annamite. I'd be interested too if I was parked ten yards to the lee of Big Mac country. That's your true Nam Memorial. Flesh, living flesh, and it's badder and madder than any stone. Ah, Big Mac. Where can I start? There are those who claim he's an ex-legionnaire who fought with the Frenchies at Dien Bien Phu. Some say he's this Marine from down Pleiku way who got busted for fragging a gung ho lieutenant. Others insist he's a blood who was at My Lai with Calley and did more than his share. But armament, now that's where the stories agree. This dude is wielding two M 16's, one in either hand, and he's got bandoliers wrapped so thick around his chest it's like he's got extra ribs. He wears grenades for earrings, and when he's angry — when he's really angry — he spits up mortar shells straight from his throat. Around his neck . . . You listening, No Dong? . . . Around his neck he wears a necklace and I don't have to tell you what it's made of. Ears, ND. Ears, the freshest and juiciest and least crinkled of which are Pol Ping's and Pol Pong's. He's Big Mac and he's hungry and he's waiting to be fed. . . . There he is now!"

Ngo Quang's heart, leaping, slammed him backward in his seat. He looked out the window and then his heart jumped again, the recoil leaving him breathless. There *was* someone out there — the old man and the young woman who had been the last visitors to leave. The expression on his face must have startled them in turn, because they immediately began to walk away, the old man fumbling open an umbrella, bringing it protectively up over the woman's head.

"Got you on that one, huh, ND? Pulse hit one fifty-three according to our infallible Yellow Peril Fear-O-Meter. This is a drill. Repeat. This is only a drill. If that had been the real Big Mac you never would have seen him. You'd be gone, a yellow smear on the mica pavement, and old Hickson here would be mouthing off for nothing, a dispatcher with no dispatchee. So I've got a stake in you, No Dong. You're the ear to my mouth, the receiver to my transmitter, my surrogate legs. . . . Yellow Peril Cabs. No terrain too hostile, no cause too lost. The Air and Space Museum? Yes, ma'am. We'll send over our closest man. . . . Hear that, ND? Haul ass. Get there in five minutes and I'll tell you the one about the VC astronaut and the Playboy bunny."

Ngo Quang had started the engine before the message came through, and now he pulled away from the sidewalk in a surge so sudden it made the tires squeal. "Atta gook! Go get her!" Hickson yelled, but it wasn't toward the Space Museum he drove, but back around in a swerving circle to a spot only a few meters from where he began. The old man and the woman stood at the edge of the sidewalk, the old man waving for a cab. A Checker peeled off from the center of the traffic and raced directly for them, but Ngo Quang had the inside track and pulled over to the curb first. He jumped out the sidewalk side and held open the door.

"We're not going far," the man said. "The Howard Johnson Motor Lodge, please."

His voice quivered just enough to show the strain he was trying to swallow. The two of them ducked past Ngo Quang into the darkness of the seat, giving him only the briefest glimpse of their features. With the woman he had the impression of someone who was in some vague way crippled. She was in her late thirties, dressed in clothes that reminded him of the USO girls he had seen in Saigon. A wife probably. Many of them still clung to the styles that had vanished with their men. Wives tended to hold themselves erect like that, too, as if sitting at attention. The man — a father? — held himself erect, as well, but in him it was more self-conscious, as if he were fitting himself to a manly model of grief.

Ngo Quang raced around to the driver's seat, turned the heat on so they wouldn't catch cold, checked the mirror to make sure they were comfortable, then gently pulled away from the curb.

"Two Ho Jo," he said into the mike. "Two Ho Jo, ten four."

"Hooray! Two live Middle Americans! ND strikes again. Give them the ride of their lives, Foo Fong. Free Vietnam never dies."

At first, they were silent, which was normal enough. The tourists, the ones who thought the war was over, would babble on about whatever attraction they were seeing next. The others, the ones who brought flowers and dog tags and little American flags, often found speech reluctant to come. It was the silence of knowing and it spread through the cab in a comforting vapor, letting Ngo Quang breathe easier than he had all night. He sat up straight in his seat to show them that he knew, too.

"Pop?" the woman said. She brought it out softly, as if testing to see whether it was time.

"Yes, Janet?"

But that was as far as she got. At the next light, Ngo

Quang was able to study her more carefully. He realized now that she wasn't crippled — that the hurt holding back he had sensed was all in her eyes.

"Pop?" she said again. "Was Mike ever here? I mean, in Washington? Did he ever get a chance to visit in high school or anything?"

The old man shook his head. "He would have liked to, but there was never time. I think he would have enjoyed the Lincoln Memorial the best."

"Or the Reflecting Pool. I think he would have liked just to lie there on the grass. I used to kid him about that, Pop. He'd see a patch of grass somewhere and go over and roll on it like a puppy. I was always scrubbing grass stains off his shirts.

"After that we could have gone to the Space Museum. He would have loved that movie they have. That carrier flight deck, too.

"And you know what else, Pop? I think he would have liked the monument. As much as he hated any kind of ceremony or anyone getting pompous, I think he would have enjoyed it. I think he would have admired the simplicity. Just those two simple walls of names."

"They take care of it so well," the old man added. "There wasn't a scrap of paper to be found."

They were silent after that. There was the smell of the old man's pipe and the softer sweetness of the woman's perfume. Ngo Quang turned the heat up higher and drove even more slowly. The pain was as alive and fresh for them as it was for him, and he wanted to express his gratitude.

The old man tapped his hand on the seat. "I haven't been in a cab in . . . let's see. Fifteen years I'll bet it's been. Not since I retired, Janet."

"It's cozy. I always wondered how they can understand

what's coming over the radio like that. It's so blurred and fast."

"That's just dispatcher talk, Janet. It's a kind of shorthand code."

Hickson was rambling on again about Big Mac, adding on more details, his voice swooping and diving like a hawk's. The buzz of it left Ngo Quang feeling dizzy and unsure. He sensed something important rested on his getting all the facts straight, but at the same time he was afraid Hickson's sarcasm would frighten off his passengers. His hand spun around the volume switch in indecision.

The old man and the woman were talking more comfortably now. Most of it concerned their flight home the next day. Departure times, transfer arrangements, schedules. When their conversation showed no sign of getting back on track, Ngo Quang decided it was time to intervene.

He tapped the rearview mirror and waited until their eyes met his. "Where?" he said.

The sound of his voice seemed to startle them. The woman rocked sideways as if he had thrown something. The old man took her arm.

"I'm sorry?" he said. "Where are we going?"

"Where?" Ngo Quang said again.

"The Howard Johnson Motor Lodge, please. I'm not sure of the address."

"I think he means . . . Do you mean where was he killed?" the woman asked.

"Where killed?" Ngo Quang said.

The man leaned forward so that his arms rested on the back of the driver's seat. "My son was killed at the battle of Dong Ha near Highway One. Do you know that area?"

"Pop," the woman began.

The old man shrugged her off. He seemed younger, more

in control than he had been just a moment before. "Do you know it? Janet, this driver is Vietnamese. It's his home. He might know Dong Ha. Do you know Dong Ha?"

Ngo Quang made a little negative motion with his head. He was disappointed, but it was worth another try. "Name?" he said.

"His name, Janet. He's asking for his name."

The woman's eyes went to the mirror. "My husband's name was Michael Petrakis. He was a second lieutenant in the U.S. Army."

Ngo Quang took the syllables in greedily. "Spell name please."

"Petrakis," the old man said. "P . . . E . . . T . . ."

But it was no use. The letters triggered no response, and when he tried to translate the sound to his fingers all he felt was an empty buzz. The old man spelled out the name three times. The woman tried once more on her own, but then the old man had his arm around her and was drawing her back against his shoulder. They sat there in silence for the rest of the ride.

"We're here," the old man said. He got out first, then helped the woman out the door. They stood for a moment under the draped yellow lights of the hotel's marquee. They seemed to stand more easily than before, as if they had managed to shrug something off in the course of the ride. The old man had his wallet out. The woman was studying an enlarged menu mounted on a sign.

"I want to thank you, sir," the old man said, coming to the window. "Here's something extra for . . ."

"Not over," Ngo Quang said quickly. He waved his hands back and forth in a crisscrossing motion.

"What's that?"

"Not over!"

The old man must have thought he was asking for more money. He kept reaching into his wallet to take out more bills, pressing them through the window until they began fluttering down against Ngo Quang's lap. He shook his head again and when the old man still didn't stop, rammed his foot down on the accelerator, speeding away.

It wasn't over. They could pretend it was, talk brave words, but things went on with an underground being. Alone, he felt the old familiar loneliness settle back on him, and he drove faster than usual to mask it. He weaved in and out of the other cars, retracing his route street by street as if by doing so he could retrace that other route, too, follow the pain right back up to its source. He didn't care if he hit anyone now. He could feel his adrenaline build like it had in the old days before an attack.

"The prodigal gook returns! Can't get rid of me that easily, No Dong. Besides, how you going to avoid Big Mac without me? Here I've been filling you in on all the salient details for the last half hour and you sit there playing Ann Landers to a couple of civilians. Bad tactics, ND. Intelligence has it that Big Mac's using K-Bar knives this week, and that's one hell of a messy way to perish. Practices on chickens, you know that? Kentucky Fried Chicken, only they ain't fried, they're raw as sushi. Keeps him sharp until a gook like you stumbles along looking to quiet the old ancestors. So bring her on home, ND. We'll get a beer, maybe stroll over to that Cambodian restaurant on Eleventh Street and break some heads. I mean a man has to flow with the times. Here we are in beautiful downtown Washington, D.C., and the leaves are falling and the nights are turning crisp and people's thoughts are turning to revenge. Revenge, Ding Dong. An eye for a toenail, a tooth for some snot. The age of revenge and getting even and settling old scores, and it's phony and rotten and stupid because there's nothing sadder than a sinner trying to get even with his own sin. But never mind that now, ND. We'll go have a drink and find a woman and it'll be like old-timey days back in Saigon. That's why you're good for me. You bring back the days when I still had a pair of legs. We were whole in those days, Ngo Quang. You and me once upon a time were pals."

Ngo Quang parked the cab in his usual spot near the walkway's start. There didn't seem to be anyone around, but he couldn't be sure. At first, he sat there casually, as if waiting for a fare, but with every passing minute he let himself sink lower in the seat until he was completely out of sight. By hunching his body up, he was able to remove his shirt, pants, and shoes. He snaked his way over to the passenger side, opened the door the barest minimum, then lowered himself down onto the sidewalk.

In some respects, it was the most exposed ten meters of all. He kept himself as low as possible, scuttling on all fours like a crab, his face close enough to the cement to feel its warmth. When he came to the edge of the mist he sprang forward as far as he could, dipping his shoulder so that his landing became a roll. He rolled a long way. When he came to a stop he was flat on his back gasping for breath. Above him he saw the arc of a mercury streetlight, and it was the same blue color of the moon on the night of the attack, so that there was no separation, and he lay there on the grass with his heart beating the same desperate way it had then.

No separation. Ahead of him were the first thin saplings, and he inched his way toward them as slowly and carefully as he had edged his way toward what the American officers had told them was the enemy bunker, willing every inch of himself deeper into the ground. On night attacks he had always felt himself illuminated in a sniper's infrared sight, and he felt exposed that same way now — as if there were cross-hairs centered on the white glowing iridescence of his head. He crawled on. In the dark, the shadows merged into a path as wide as his body, and he was able to make the next band of shrubbery in relatively fast time. He rested there, listening to the distant hum of the radio and Hickson's unintelligible voice. Under it was another sound that was much vaguer, a cross between an amused little snort and the surprised rustle of a bird. It seemed to come mixed with the carbon smell of a doused campfire, and it was alluring and frightening at the same time.

Ngo Quang crawled on. He could see the monument now in the gaps between bushes. It was sunk below the level of the grass like the sandbagged foxhole he had stumbled upon when he had lost the rest of his platoon. The lights seemed to have been dimmed since earlier in the night. He could just make out the golden letters on the monument's walls, but they were still hazy, and the only impression he had was of their mass.

There were only twenty meters left to go. The carbon smell was gone now, but in its place was something that made him rub his nose in alarm. Marijuana. Pungent, sweet, unmistakable. It wafted toward him from the thick interior of the mist, and it came accompanied by a hoarse and bitter laugh. He detoured to his right to get away from it, but as he did so his trailing foot brushed against something brittle and cold. Carefully, his nerves rigid in anticipation, he reached back his hand.

Chicken bones. Mounds of them. Crunched and mangled and piled in ugly heaps. Chicken bones with flesh still on them, reeking of death. Chicken bones arranged in the long tapering shape of a man's corpse.

Ngo Quang jumped to his feet and started racing across

the exposed walkway just as he had jumped up and raced toward the foxhole on the night of the attack. The laugh was right behind him, chattering away like a machine gun, and he swerved from side to side to avoid it, throwing himself headfirst toward the place on the monument where the two walls met. There were shadows there. In their protection he stood up and began rubbing his hands across the names.

He ran them fast, stretching up as far as he could, bringing his fingers down the middle, fanning them out, and groping back again, trying to find the warm mating pulse that would spell out the name of the soldier he had killed. He remembered crawling the last few meters to the foxhole, the surprised look on the soldier's face as he lay there behind the sandbags, the way he said "Huh?" as if someone had just asked him a question, the way they had simultaneously reached for their guns. When Ngo Quang's had gone off first it was as if the bullets were outracing the truth, smashing everything apart, not only his bullets but all the bullets and shells and bombs ever fired, so that the fragments were still flying dangerously through the night, still looking for targets to mutilate and destroy. He remembered crawling over to the dying soldier, fingering the sticky blood of his shoulder, trying to prod him back to life with the butt of his gun.

He ran his hands across the highest line of names, then the line of names below that, then the one below that, but there were so many his palms became blistered, his arms began spasming from the strain. Behind him he could hear footsteps, heavy boots cracking down against pebbles, the metallic snap of a magazine being rammed home. A flashlight beam found the edge of the monument, then began sweeping closer in overlapping circles, searching him out.

Behind the beam was a separate flashing that seemed to hover in the blackness like the laugh, silver and sharp, and it was this that panicked him most of all.

"Friend!" Ngo Quang yelled. "ARVN, Big Mac! ARVN!" The wall was tapering, the lines of names coming to an end. The smell of marijuana was overpowering now, and his head began to swim from the sweetness. He reached down to run his hands across the last row, groped for it the same desperate way he had groped for the dog tags, but then his hands were freed from their groping by stronger hands and brought away from the stone. There was a sucking sound, the kind a throat wound makes. There was a moist puffing against the loose skin at the base of his ear.

Ngo Quang felt regret but no fear. The hands fastened on his wrists and lifted them up toward his chest. He struggled for a moment, but the hands were too strong for him, and by the time they forced his own hands to his own throat, he felt nothing but a warm anesthetized calm. Not over, he wanted to say, but the air wasn't there for it, and so he closed his eyes and looked into the darkness and swallowed the bitter retching phlegm of the end.

Back on the curb, Hickson's voice burst through static.

"Just the first, ND. You lead the way and thousands will follow until we have a whole army of gook cabbies, nothing but gooks, sin chauffeuring sin — can't you see it? Yellow Peril Cab here. No terrain too hostile, no cause too lost. What's that, sir? A driver who knows this city like the back of his proverbial hand? Hang on for a second and we'll send over our best man."

The Mall: A History

IT'S HARD to go shopping without thinking of the end of the world. The malls with their sterile fountains jetting up to heights that always collapse six or seven inches below true joy. The piped-in music too sticky to inhale. The concrete terraces between stores with their plastic benches and plastic kiosks and the kind of frequent cover that mass murderers find convenient. The confused eighty-year-olds searching for the lost and found so they can turn themselves in. The bored kids in obnoxious clothes, playing at hostility with the security guards, pathetically dependent on their anger. The shoppers, the affluent shoppers clearing spaces for themselves with the hard beams of their expressions, animals high enough up on the consumption chain for arrogance, but not so high that insecurity doesn't make them rush the cash registers to get there first. Seeing all this, seeing the cheap and tacky disguised as the valuable and good, the pretense and artificiality, it's hard not to long for a surgically delivered nuclear strike.

"You're exaggerating," my sister said as we left the Bagel Knosh and went into Mr. Pants. "You're always exaggerating." She thought about it for a moment, then corrected herself. "You have been exaggerating since you were ten."

Truth comes to me like that, in big dollops that make me want to inflate my vision to keep up. Linda gets her truth the opposite way, in tiny increments that have to wedge into the indisputability of what she already knows. We cancel out each other's biases. Her common sense is about the only thing strong enough to make me return to Long Island. Remembering how much I hate the place does a lot to soften the brunt of an Adirondack winter.

"You're becoming a hick," she said, looking me over. "It's time you bought clothes that were lined with something besides reindeer."

We left Mr. Pants and went over to Mr. Chinos. Linda bought some Christmas presents for her boys. I had it in my mind that what I really needed wasn't pants but a ball of twine. Coarse, simple twine. The good sense and honesty of my quest would lead me past the bare-breasted mannequins and sultry salesgirls and let me emerge unscathed on the other side.

"Is there a stationery store around here?" I asked, tugging on her sleeve.

Linda shops like a drunk on a pub crawl. Every store encountered is a store entered, and there's no holding her back. We went into Undies Unlimited to price Merry Widows.

"I don't think you're enjoying yourself," she said, in a tone that meant she wasn't. "Do I complain when I go up there and you take me searching for blueberries in a corrupt, polluted swamp?"

"I hate malls."

"I know you hate malls. But they have their bright spots. They do a lot of good."

"Name one thing."

She was ready for me. "They give old people a place to go."

It's amazing how many abominations are excused because of old people. TV, fast-food franchises, malls. They're ruining this country, turning people's brains into mush, but it's okay, in fact it's fantastic, because they give old people a place to go. For centuries heaven and hell were palmed off on us for the same reason.

"What I really hate," I continued, "even more than the conspicuous consumption and forced jollity and the ethos that permits teenagers to tote around credit cards, what I really hate besides these is the climate control, the complete expulsion of fresh air. Take a deep breath. No, a *deep* breath. See? You can't even get half a lungful without coughing."

"It's the cigarette smoke."

"It's the vaporization of greed and it's fatal. Even birds get it. Look over there."

A starling was flying around with a piece of hot dog bun, trying desperately to find its way outside. It was like watching a fly on a window, only on a larger scale. The bird butted and probed, chipped and pecked, but the glass was inescapable, and after a while it settled onto a beam and merely shivered. Linda, who is sentimental about animals, was visibly moved.

"It'll be dead in an hour," I said, sensing I had her on the ropes. "Mall air is poisonous. Malls kill several million birds a year."

"You made that up," she said, not quite ready to give in.

"Several million. You don't know that."

"I'm a historian," I told her. "I get paid to know."

My talents in history and exaggeration were developed at the same time and place: the suburban Long Island of 1959. Stewart School, built in the Thirties, was and still is the most beautiful elementary school there. The town it serves had an easy Depression, and between cheap construction costs and an aristocratic bias, they ended up building something that was as close as you could get in America to Eton and still be in a public school. The Georgian architecture with its understated crenellation. The beautifully manicured playing fields set beside a small lake. The voluminous library with its bay windows of stained glass. Going to school there *compelled* you to be interested in history. Those were the remote days when George Washington's portrait hung in all the classrooms, and we naturally assumed it was because it had once been his home.

The school's roof played a part, too. It was flat, flat enough to act as magnet for tennis balls, soccer balls, and the hats of the homelier girls. I was appointed roof monitor in fifth grade. In our frisky class, I was one of the few who could be trusted to sweep off the debris without falling over.

You could see a lot of history from that roof, especially Long Island history, which is what we were studying that year. The Rainbow Division monument on the site of old Camp Mills. The Cathedral of the Incarnation built by the school's namesake, A. T. Stewart, inventor of the department store. The remains of the famous Vanderbilt Motorway to Oyster Bay. Mitchell Field and its DC-3's. These were all in range.

There were things I couldn't see, of course. Trends, movements, and such. Invisible things. Things the houses, walls, and trees all hid. Thus I completely missed the growing emancipation of women from household chores and child-raising, the gradual influx of black people into what had heretofore been all-white preserves, the brew of evil currents that would result in Kennedy's assassination, the expansion of colleges and schools to make room for the baby-boomers, the increasing importance of the computer, and the growth of American arrogance that was to have its comeuppance in Vietnam. The roof just wasn't that high.

That was one problem with history. It hadn't happened yet. The other problem was that it had already happened, and I had missed it. I wanted to be a historian of things that were happening *now*, in 1959. So I kept my eyes open. For most of the fall nothing particularly historic happened, and when it did Tommy Chu was the one to spot it first.

Tommy was the shortest boy in fifth grade, but something of a dynamo. "The Chinese Chopstick" we called him — he was skinny and tough. What I remember him mostly doing is jumping. He would jump over desks and onto desks and out of trees and into trees. There was so much energy in his small frame that he needed to expend a certain amount of the surplus merely to remain at sea level. It was a wonder the teachers trusted him on the roof. Mike Manning and I would stay in the center near the exhaust ducts, dozing in the soft November sun, conserving our energy for adulthood, but Tommy was always teetering on the edge.

"Hey, look over there!" he shouted. "Jesus Christ, look at that! Will you look and see what's over there! My God, I don't believe what I'm seeing over there! Will you get a load of that there over there!"

He had to do this for about half an hour before we got up. When we joined him he was pointing toward the most historic quarter of the horizon, the flat sandy plain that had once been Roosevelt Field, the spot Lindbergh had taken off from to cross the Atlantic. It was less than a mile from the school, but with only a hangar or two left I preferred to exercise my imagination in busier directions.

What he was pointing at was less a sight than a sound — a deep heavy grumbling. After a while it materialized into a cloud of dust that was similar to leaf smoke, only browner. Beneath the cloud like a rusty stirrer was a huge red crane.

"They're building something!" Tommy yelled.

Mike — who had brains, strength and talent, and a sarcastic streak I couldn't figure out — was not impressed. "You're a genius, Chu. They're building something. Twang your magic twanger."

"What in hell is it?" I said, playing peacemaker.

All during the winter whatever it was took on more form. What I remember most is how verticality was gradually established on what I had always thought of as unending horizontalness. You're a kid, you think the world goes on forever, then one day you butt into a wall and infinity stops rolling. Before, I had thought that by looking toward Roosevelt Field I was looking toward Paris — that by squinting or using binoculars I could make out the Arc de Triomphe. I didn't think that anymore. My eyes banged to a stop against two matching five-story buildings that were as square and featureless as anything I had ever seen.

I don't know who used the right word first. Mike was smartest, so let's credit it to him.

"It's a mall," he said one afternoon in March.

"A malted milk," Tommy giggled.

"What's a mall?" I said.

We decided to find out. It was the work of five seconds to run down the fire escape and mount our Schwinns. There were several games of soccer base in progress on the playground, but we avoided them all and made directly for our secret route, the old Vanderbilt Road. It had been used for the first road races in America back at the turn of the century, but there wasn't much left now except for chunky bits of concrete and patchy, overgrown ruts. We walked our bikes over the rougher stretches. Tommy kept putting his down to jump up on tree stumps, beat his fists against his chest, and leap off.

"There's a squirrel," Mike said, pointing toward the road's scrubby marge.

For a moment we thought we had him. "A squirrel," Tommy said. "That's terrific, Manning. You're just like Marlin Perkins or something. Why don't you go lasso his tail?"

Mike didn't usually allow remarks like this to pass, but he did this time. He rubbed his head to show he was thinking, then jerked his thumb the other way. "There's a rabbit."

Rabbits being scarcer than squirrels, we looked to where he pointed. Sure enough there was a rabbit, a brown trembling nothing. And not just one rabbit, but two rabbits. Two rabbits, then three rabbits, then five squirrels, then a *fox*, then so many small animals we lost count. They were running past us through the underbrush with a definite air of panic, as though being chased by flames.

"What goes on?" Tommy whined.

I had no idea. Mike, though, continued thinking.

"They're migrating," he said at last. "These are migrating animals."

Migrating from what? We walked on a little more cautiously. The roadway became fainter the farther along it we went, and disappeared completely in another hundred yards. There was a bare patch of dirt to cross, then we were on the brand-new approach road that had been bulldozed through the animals' domain. We could see better from here. Ahead on the left was a high white building with the word GIM-

BEL'S on the top. There on the right was a similar building
with an equally big sign: MACY'S. In between stretched
some lower, more nondescript buildings and a bunch of
empty foundations. There were all kinds of earth-moving
machines and cranes and so on, so we couldn't see everything. What impressed us most started right there at our
feet.

"Holy shit!" Tommy yelled. "The ocean!"

Stretching as far as we could see was an unbroken expanse
of blue pavement — the biggest, most immense parking lot
we had ever seen or even thought about, a parking lot so big
it restored all my notions of infinity in one awe-inspiring
flash. Mike had us kneel down at the edge and lean our
heads against it. For the first time I was able to see the actual
curve of the earth.

It was terrifying in its way. Terrifying and funny. What
was especially funny was that it was practically empty. The
only cars we could see were in a little circle over there by
Macy's, their hoods pointed into the wind like fishing boats
riding out a storm. It was such a terrible miscalculation it
made us laugh. All those parking spaces and only eight cars!
How stupid could they get!

We raced our bikes across the pavement. Macy's was our
first stop — we knew the name from the Thanksgiving pa-
rade on TV. Though the store was open, we didn't go in, but
walked around the circumference staring in the windows,
trying to make sense of it all. To me, department stores were
musty places where clerks held their sleeves up with elastic
bands and delivered messages to each other through pneumatic tubes. They were historic. They were 1958. Macy's,
on the other hand, was 1959. The escalators crossing in
bright, elegant X's, the mannequins spinning on electrified
turntables, the glitter and flash. Indisputably 1959.

We walked around it five times. Every few feet was a wet puddle of concrete and some roped-off trees. There was a lot of steel around, too. Fresh orange girders, fresh orange beams. It was as if America's entire industrial output were being poured down a narrow chute with the mall at its end.

By our sixth circumnavigation, the enchantment had slackened enough for us to break away. We started down an open sidewalk toward Gimbel's, our heads bent into our chests to make progress against the wind. There were other stores along the way, most of them decorated with red, white, and blue bunting, and signs that read *Grand Opening!* Walgreen's Drug Store, Hallmark Cards, Davega's Sporting Goods. They weren't continuous, but separated by foundations where other stores were being built. Up above us men in hard hats tiptoed across beams no wider than seesaws, risking death with every step. It lent a sense of adventure to the humdrum stores — there was a melodramatic moment when I decided the bunting was to commemorate the laborers who had sacrificed their lives during construction.

"So where's the mall thing?" Tommy wanted to know.

"A mall is a shaded walkway or public promenade," Mike said. He was famous for studying dictionaries. "This is a mall we're walking on. Someday these shops will all be linked."

We continued exploring. There was a water fountain that didn't work, a map that was mostly blank, a monument marking the spot where the *Spirit of St. Louis* had lifted off the runway back in 1927. Few of the shops on that end of the mall were open yet, and the ones that were had little in the way of either customers or merchandise. Some were wildly inappropriate for the setting (a diaper supply service; a glorified pawnshop); others were a decade and more ahead of their time (a store that sold nothing but bagels). It was obvious that a great deal of trial and error had to be gone through before the weaker businesses weeded themselves out. In the meantime, the salesclerks stood by the doors with their hands behind their backs, patiently waiting. Everything seemed like it was waiting. The unlit neon signs, the quiet cash registers. Waiting for what, I wasn't sure. Waiting for things to decide what they were going to be. Waiting the way a blank wall waits for a coat of new paint. Waiting like my brain when I opened a new book. An energetic waiting. It made me a lot more excited about the future than I had been in quite a while.

We were almost back to Macy's when we came upon the pizza stand. To us, pizza was still a relatively new snack, and not knowing how to eat it, we each tried a different style. Tommy held his slice up to his chin like a washcloth and wiped it back and forth across his tongue. Mike rolled his up like a cigarette and sucked casually on the tip. I flapped mine back and forth to cool it, then yanked it apart like taffy.

There was a bench in front. We sat there talking things over.

"You know something?" I said. "This mall thing. I think it has potential."

"I think it stinks," Tommy said.

Mike looked at me with new respect. "Yeah. Potential. I was just thinking the same thing."

I was flattered by his agreement, and it made me talk even faster. "I mean, you know how when you go shopping and you have to keep getting in a car and going all over the place? Here you drive up and leave your car and you can walk up and down and it's like being in a miniature city. A miniature city is what this is. People can come and stroll around and sit and talk and it's great. I mean, this is something that really could be the wave of the future."

I was pretty proud of myself for thinking of it in those terms. Tommy acted confused and started doing jumping jacks, but Mike was quick to add a few points of his own.

"They could have dances and things. They could have lectures by famous experts eminent in their fields. Kids who didn't want to go shopping could sit out here and play. It would be like a new community."

"Yeah, a new community," I said. "They could build apartments for old people on top of the stores and they could ride the escalators down to shop. They could build a small farm or something in between stores. The whole mall could be self-supporting."

"It's too cold," Tommy said, anxious to spoil things.

It was then that Mike came up with his best idea. "They could enclose it," he said. "They could make a gigantic bubble that would keep out the cold air."

"Okay, stupid. What about summer?"

"Air-conditioning. It would be a cinch."

The concept was so new and obviously brilliant we felt we should go tell some adult. We walked around for a while without finding anyone who looked like he was in a position to do anything about it, so we tried the last row of stores. We didn't expect it to be much different from the rest of the mall, but it *was* different — dramatically different. The sound for one thing. Instead of the pounding of pneumatic drills there was the lilt of amplified music. There was a waltz and a pleasant clicking sort of noise that underlined the beat. As usual, Mike identified it first.

"Ice skates."

We hurried on. There in the very center of the concrete

was an oval expanse of white ice. Around the perimeter ran a blue board draped with overcoats and scarves. In the middle of the rink a skating class was in progress, with a dozen or so girls. They were older than us, but not by much, and most of them giggled when they saw us watching. Some nonchalant high schoolers stood waiting their turn by the warming shed, and behind them was a group of parents blowing on the rims of paper cups.

I'm not sure whether it was the clean, unexpected circle of ice, the fact that it was the only place we had found with definite signs of activity, or simply the leotarded beauty of the girls, but we were immediately enthralled. It was as if the potential of the mall, a second after we had sensed it, had been gloriously fulfilled. An ice rink! What a great idea!

"I like the blonde," Mike said, pointing his thumb. "Give me a tight little ass every time."

He was way ahead of us on that, too. To me in my innocence they looked like a band of particularly agile and graceful angels going through their warmups prior to descending to earth. I'm not sure what Tommy thought of them. Any display of energy triggered off his own, and he was hopping from one leg to another to blow off steam.

We stayed there until they finished practicing, then stayed on to watch the older girls. It was dark by the time they finished. After a miniature tractor went over the ice to smooth it down, a single skater came out by herself and glided to a stop in the cross of spotlights. She was our age and gorgeous. It wasn't just her Betty Boop figure or long auburn hair or pouty red lips, though these contributed. It was her smile — her bright, warm, semi-approachable semi-aloof Mouseketeer smile. Gorgeous. She took off her jacket, leaned over to pull off her warmup pants, then with a glorious turning motion launched into her routine.

To say she was a brilliant skater would be to do her an injustice. She was skating incarnate. Her coach leaned on the boards calling out instructions over the music, but he may as well have been coaching a bird. She danced over that rink like a happy froth the ice was churning up to gladden our hearts. Those backward glides and dainty stretches. Those humorous little skips and breathtaking pirouettes. How easy she made them look! Just when I had decided it was impossible for anything that graceful to remain landbound, she took to the air, in long extravagant leaps that left hollow spaces in my stomach. Her hair flowed behind her like a velvet marker tracing where she had been; her skates threw up shavings of ice that showered our heads and made us shiver. We wanted to applaud her, leap over the boards and join her there on the ice, collapse on our knees to kiss her skates, but before we could she came to a sudden stop, put her hands above her head as if she were about to hoist herself into heaven, folded them in tight to her body, and began to spin, spinning faster, spinning so fast that her shape became a blur that seemed to take in everything — the coldness of the night, the promise of it all, the potential we were so aware of in ourselves and the mall and in 1959.

All three of us had erections by the time she finished. Mine wasn't sexual, but a longing for something I didn't even know I wanted until then. A longing for . . . Well, longing. I wanted to long. I wanted to want something so badly and with such fervor that it was impossible to achieve. At the center of my life I wanted the ungraspable. I wanted her.

Mike was the one who recovered his voice first. "What a knockout," he sighed.

"Ethereal," I added.

"Annette Funicello," Tommy said.

We came back the following night, then the night after that, then every night for a week. She started with the same basic routine every time, so we soon learned her patterns, and our stomachs would butterfly in anticipation every time another leap came due. Now and then she would fall, but not awkwardly, and the pity we felt for her as she furiously brushed the ice away from her short red skirt only made us love her all the more. Suzy was her name. Her coach would call her over to the boards and sketch diagrams on a blackboard he propped against his arm. But she must have been a difficult pupil to teach. As faithfully as she tried to follow out his instructions, there was a wild, rebellious something in her that made her keep improvising on her own.

"We've got to talk to her," Mike insisted. "Find out her last name. Find out where she goes to school."

"Then what?" Tommy said.

We decided not to worry about that part yet. It would be enough just getting near enough to say hello. To speak during her routine would have been sacrilege, but we had a better solution anyway. We had noticed that once her practice session was over, she would linger on for the public skating, a public skating that was of course open to anyone. Anyone, that is, with skates.

"We'll rent them," Tommy suggested.

Mike shook his head. "They don't rent them here. I already checked."

"We can buy them," I said. "We can go into Davega's, buy some skates, then we'll skate up to her and then boom."

"Boom what?" Tommy asked.

"Boom nothing. Boom your head."

"We don't know how to skate."

"We'll learn."

I spent all weekend raking leaves to earn enough money.

My hands became blistered and my wrists bled from thorns, but whenever I thought of Suzy's hair and the way it streamed behind her as she flew across the rink, I only raked faster. Tommy came over on Sunday to help. Between raking and our savings we had just enough for skates. Mike had enough money, too, but when we asked him how he had earned it, he was evasive.

"Stuff," he mumbled.

"What kind of stuff?" I asked.

"Easy stuff." He leered at us the way he did when he cheated in math. "I stole it. My old man keeps some cash in a sock beneath the couch. I stole it, okay? Everyone steals."

Once school was over we raced our bikes to the mall. Mike stealing money like that seemed to spoil things somehow, color what should have been a bright orange something into a dull, murky brown. So I was apprehensive right from the start. We reached Davega's just before closing. I picked out a pair of black figure skates, deciding it was the only way to keep up with her, but Tommy and Mike both went for the leaner, more rakish-looking hockey ones. We wobbled around the carpet trying them on, fell down, then yanked each other back up again. It didn't matter. We were in such a rush to get onto the ice with her we would have gone barefoot.

The salesman wrapped up the skates for us. The moment we got outside we tore the wrapping off, tied the laces together, draped them over our shoulders blade-side-out, then ran like mad for the rink. At first Mike was ahead, but Tommy knew a shortcut, and he had raced past us and was lengthening his lead when he suddenly stumbled. He ran to his right, stopped, ran to his left, stopped again. It was so abrupt we nearly piled into him.

"What's the matter, clown!" Mike yelled.

"Wrong turn," Tommy mumbled. He rubbed his mitten across his face. "The rink's not here."

"Are you blind or something? There it is right down . . ."

Mike's hand, his arrogant, pointing hand, went flabby and collapsed to his side. "Oh Jesus no," he whispered.

The ice rink was gone. The ice, the blue boards surrounding it, the warming shed, the girls. They were gone. In its place was a round white building shaped like a wheel of Swiss cheese. A crane towered above its center — a cable ran down to the roof, showing how it had been lowered into place. One side of the building opened in a wedge with a door. MR. CHEEZIT read the sign. GRAND OPENING TODAY!

I don't think we said anything, not at first. We stumbled toward it in silence, the excitement in our stomachs souring into something that was mushy and cold. I remember being terribly self-conscious about my skates, twisting them around behind me so no one could see. There were some ticket stubs for public skating scattered on the cement. It was the only evidence left.

We walked into the entrance. There were cheeses hanging from the ceiling and cheeses piled up on the floor. We went up to the cash register. The salesman was dressed like a mouse.

"What happened to the ice rink?" I asked him.

"What ice rink?" he sneered, staring right over me. His whiskers reeked of tobacco.

"There was an ice rink here. Last Friday. There were these classes."

"I don't know nothing about no ice rink. Beat it, punks."

"You eat too much cheese, mister," Mike said. "It oozes out your ears."

The salesman yelled at us to get out. We left, but on our way to the door Mike drove the dirty tip of his shoe into one of the cheese wheels and twisted it so there was a big hole.

We didn't know what to do after that. We felt cheated, and not sure of what. We sat on a bench for a while. We went into Macy's and Mike stole a fountain pen. We walked up to Gimbel's and Tommy stole a scarf. We ate some pizza. Mike took his pen and scribbled *skating sucks* on the side of the Lindbergh monument. We didn't talk about the girl or the cheese shop or our disappointment. Mostly what we did was hang around.

There's a sequel to this. I don't mean the sequel of high school when we went to the mall when there was nothing else to do. I don't mean the sequel of Tommy's life, his drifting through college to evade the draft, his series of jobs with different banks, his marriages, the way his skin became creased, how he seemed to perceptibly shrink as he neared thirty and his energy dried up. I don't mean the sequel of Mike's life either, how he turned his brains and cynicism into running a public-relations firm that specialized in ad campaigns for foreign dictators. I don't even mean my own sequel, my associate professorship at a third-rate college whose name no one can pronounce, my career as a historian who can't let facts be but must pump them up to match his own requirements. And I don't mean the sequel of our generation, our generation without accomplishment, our generation that is *all* sequel and anticlimax and nostalgia and regret.

What I refer to is a party I attended at Columbia in 1968. I was the only person there who wasn't stoned silly, and I was pretty close. Sitting next to me was a girl my age who could have passed for forty, so badly used did she appear by life. She was still rather attractive, though, and she wore an indecently short corduroy skirt. The man sitting next to her had taken advantage of her condition to place his hand on her right leg. When he got up to get a fresh joint I put my hand where his had been. The girl gave me a vivid smile, but her eyes didn't focus.

"Hey, I know you from somewhere," I said.

"Sure, sure," she mumbled. "Got a light?"

She had auburn hair. It was dirty and scraggly, but even so . . . "Were you a skater?" I asked.

"Oh, yeah, yeah. Skating. Yeah, a very big deal."

"I remember you. Where they put that cheese shop in. You had private skating lessons. You used to start off with spins and finish off with jumps."

She smiled like an orphan who's suddenly been recognized as a missing princess. "That was me!" she said. "I was Suzy! Yes, I was Suzy. It's me, Suzy!"

She said it so many times she started crying. I reached into my pocket for a hanky, but there wasn't one, so I handed her some rolling paper instead. "I was Suzy," she sniffed, dabbing her eyes.

"Jesus, that was a long time ago," I said. I couldn't think of anything else to say. The moment her friend came back with the joint, I got up and left.

A long time ago. When I asked my sister where Mr. Cheezit was, she stared at me like I was insane. "Never heard of it," she said.

"But it was right around here somewhere," I insisted. "Right where the skating rink was."

"Before Croissant King? I think there used to be a tie store here, but that was aeons ago." She made a face and pointed to where some teenagers sat twisting each other's hair into spikes. "Look at them," she said. "It's one thing I do have against malls, I'll grant you that. All they do is loiter around and cause trouble. I mean, it's like a day-care center for juvenile delinquents. Don't they have anything better to do than hang out?"

"You're looking at the man who invented it," I told her.

She gave me one of her realistic looks. To the left of Croissant King was a store called Threads and Patches that sold twine, only it wasn't twine but synthetic plastic cord. *TwinTwine* was the name. *The Twine That Binds.* When I got home to the country I used it to fasten a bird feeder to my porch. The first chickadee to sit on it tore it in half.

Antediluvian Man

Ex-priest, that was easy, little more than the shrug that rolled the thin cotton blanket off his shoulders to the floor. A yearning sometimes for solitude, a pious cast to his voice, the unbreakable habit of waking up like this before dawn. Ex-congressman, that was harder, a rough spot up there near the pillows, a tendency to choke them in the sour dregs of his dreams. "I am choking ignorance," he explained to Christina the first time she had caught him at it. "I am choking a member from Louisiana with a greenish boil on his nose standing by the speaker's desk calling me a Communist tool." Occasionally, he hurled the pillows toward the wall, and Christina would carry them back to bed cradled in either arm like the babies he couldn't give her. An aftertaste of power, a thickness in his middle, an undeserved reputation as a man of affairs. Ex-husband, that was the tough one, no Christina to fetch his pillows, no Christina to rearrange his blankets, no Christina to smooth away the scars and disappointments from the other ex's of his life.

A craving for warmness. A need for stroking. A whisper he listened for that was no longer there.

Unbearable, he decided, reaching out for her missing form. He let his hand linger on the sheet that was damp from his sweat, then brought it back in a violent gesture toward the radio alarm. It had gone off now. He fumbled for the switch, then gave up and lay there motionless suffering the news. A plane crash in Kyoto had killed three hundred and twenty-six. The price of gold was higher. Diabetes had been successfully introduced in rats. He listened to all three stories, waiting for word of the rally, the brief mention of his name. Tomorrow they could expect full treatment, two minutes at least, a snippet from the speeches, token chanting, the usual underestimation of the numbers that were there. But today the mere announcement would have been enough, and when the rats were followed by the weather he felt the vague slackening in his stomach that served as his premonition of doom.

"The heat wave continues in Boston, with record temperatures forecast for the eighth straight day."

The humidity jumped him the moment he sat up. At first, he was tempted to let himself fall back again onto the coolness of the sheets, then with a decisive straightening he pushed himself up, crossed the carpet to the window, and pulled up the shade. The sun had already blasted away the subtle shadings that made city life bearable. The leaves on the tree before the apartment were shriveled into themselves like morning glories in reverse. The grass of the mall down Commonwealth Avenue was patchy and brown. A few joggers raced the heat, but they were panting, slowing, coming reluctantly to a stop. Other mornings their energy would mirror his own, even increase it, but now their weariness sapped what little strength he had left. When he attempted breakfast, it was all he could do to scrape off the cereal from the side of the bowl.

The hell with it. He wouldn't go to the rally. He would go to the beach with the mob.

To the beach! He said it out loud, picturing its effect on the eager faces that would be staring up at him waiting for their orders to march. Sixty thousand sweating activists parading down Route 3 towel-in-hand, oblivious to concerns of megatons and warheads and nuclear winters, seeking only to douse their bodies in the nearest patch of cool surf. The image of it made him feel good for a moment, then the inevitable reaction set in. A hot, muggy morning in the life of a divorced fifty-year-old man, and here he was ready to trade in the convictions of a lifetime for one self-indulgent afternoon.

Ex-believer in the human race?

That was the big one, the sum total of the other ex's, a fit topic for meditation as he sat there forcing harsh bran down his throat. His years as a priest had given him professional familiarity with the state of his soul, and it didn't take him long to check on its current status. The pity was still there. The generalized pity that took in no one specific but lay inside him like a tender magnet, ready to clutch any stray need that came his way. The force he felt in his voice was there, too, the eloquence that came from his loins, his sense of manhood. The selfish delight he took in its ability to sway people, the completeness he only found when its urgency enlisted the separate pities of a crowd. These things were still there, and so was the mercy that tempered it, made him human. Power was the cancer of his times, yet in him it bred its own antibodies, so that reaching a critical mass of influence he would cut and run. Archbishop of Boston, senator from Massachusetts, partner in a marriage that was the envy of his friends. These were all possibilities he had fled from, and still power came back to him, and here he was on the verge of fleeing yet again.

Ex-believer in the human race? Not yet, not so strong that he would stay home on a whim. He showered and dressed, blaming his reluctance on the divorce. The evidence was everywhere. The mail in her name waiting to be forwarded, her abandoned clothes, the smell of talcum. Exhibits of his staleness, and he spent the rest of the morning cleaning up. By the time he had thrown out the last bottle of perfume, destroyed her stationery, swept every hair from every pillow, hunted down her books on male infertility and ripped them into shreds, he was sweating like a lumberjack, but the slackened, helpless feeling was still there.

Major surgery, he decided, taking a sardonic pleasure in the phrase. A new apartment. A new city, a start somewhere else. But these were long-term solutions, and there was still the rally to worry about. A quicker change was needed to get him through the next few days. Ten years ago he would have gone on a retreat in the mountains; five years ago, he would have recaptured his energy in the kind of grueling committee work the other congressmen couldn't stand. Neither expedient was possible now. His staleness needed something newer, something he had never tried before.

He looked across the room toward the phone. One of Christina's slips was draped over the chair to its left. The frilliest edge blew in a draft from the fan, matching his irony with irony of its own. The phone and the lace were the same shade of blue. Their juxtaposition suggested something that was amusing and arousing at the same time. Passionate undressings, stolen conversations — an affair. An affair of lust unadorned with affection. It would be just the thing.

Only now that the impulse had crystallized did he realize the temptation had been in his head for over a week. It had been a dinner indistinguishable from a thousand others. The lavish introduction, the standard speech, the programs handed him to autograph, the pressing of hands. As usual, some of the women had hung on the fringes of the crowd, waiting to speak to him alone. As usual, one had made it clear she was interested in him in a capacity beyond his being chairman of the Stop War Now group. "You're such a warm man," they usually began. "So much more human-looking than on TV." The difference was that this time he had regarded the girl who said it with something other than the gentlemanly indifference that was his usual defense. Young, he remembered thinking. So young and beautiful to be offering herself to a tired man like me.

She had written her phone number on a napkin. When he refused to take it, she had tucked it into his jacket pocket. "There," she said, letting her hand linger on his arm. "Just in case you ever need someone to listen." He fumbled through his papers for it now, trying desperately to come up with her name. Ruth, Esther. Something Old Testament enough to have made him laugh.

He felt a rush of adrenaline as the phone rang, the boyish kind, and it made him hesitate a bit when a man answered the phone.

"Hello?"

Mother of God. He took a deep breath. "Hello, this is Thomas Beston calling," he said.

The man — her husband, he assumed — seemed delighted at the news. "Father Tom! Hey, what a surprise. Rachel said you might be calling. She'll be sorry she missed you."

"She's out then?"

"Did you want to leave a message or anything?"

The man's voice was ridiculously young. He sounded like a salesman of some kind, all eagerness and good cheer.

"Well, no, there's really no message. I just wanted to . . ."

"Talk to her about that meeting? She wants you to address that group of Mount Holyoke grads she's involved with about this peace-kick thing."

It was absurd, he couldn't quite believe it, but there it was all laid out for him. The naive husband, the ready-made excuse, a prefabricated affair set to go.

"Well, yes," he said, deepening his voice. "Yes, I would like very much to meet with her to go over our plans."

"Can I tell you something, Father Tom? You were the best congressman this district ever had, no lie. I voted for you three times. Watching you chew out those generals was the best show on TV. When you going to run again?"

Absurd, he thought. He was trying to find a graceful way to disengage himself when there was a plastic clicking sound. A woman's voice came on, talking under her breath.

"It's for me, Richard. I'll take it now."

"Hi, hon. Didn't hear you come in. You'll never guess in a zillion years who's calling."

"I'll take it," she said, this time with an edge to her tone.

The husband hung up.

"Father Tom?" she whispered. "Hold on for a second. I want to make sure the door is closed."

A thirty-second phone call, and already he felt like he had been sneaking in and out of bed for twenty years.

"I thought I'd call," he said when she came back on. "I thought I'd take you up on your offer to listen."

"I knew it," she said, laughing so softly it was almost a purr. He tried to picture what she looked like, but again all he came up with was a generalized sense of her availability and youth.

"When?" he said.

"This afternoon. Richard will be home watching the Red Sox. I could meet you somewhere."

"I'm speaking at the rally."

"What rally?"

"On the Common. It's been forty years."

"Forty years?"

"Since Hiroshima."

She went on as if she hadn't heard him. "At two. There's a place called the Green Parrot off the exit in Braintree. I'll meet you there."

"Yes, that would be great. Only I have this little matter of the rally. I'm the keynote speaker and all. Very important stuff."

"Oh, I think you'll come," she said. This time her voice was huskier. It was as if she had just reached out and touched him on the thigh.

Things had gone far enough. "Listen, Rachel. I have certain responsibilities. There are issues so large that neither you nor I nor anyone can willfully —"

"You'll come," she said, and with that she clicked down the phone.

The humidity was even worse in the Public Garden than it was on the street. Tents of brown mist enveloped each tree, and the air had a heavy, poisonous feel, as if it were the exhalation of the surrounding cement. He shouldered his way through the weight of it, forcing himself up a path he remembered as running downhill. In the antiwar days, he would walk to a rally this way and feel himself being funneled into a larger purpose the way a drop is funneled into a stream. All the separateness would merge, the crowd would tighten, people would start to hold hands, until finally they marched in an irresistible surge up the Common, deploying around the speaker's stand in the overflowing glory of their strength.

In the old days. Everything was different then. People wore dungarees, overalls, army fatigues — clothes that may have been affected, but were at least meant for work. Today they were more apt to wear jogging clothes or shorts, making it seem as if the rally were just one more recreation in their recreation-packed days.

He could live with it — as long as they came. He rested for a moment by the swan boats, trying for an early estimate of the crowd's size. It was hard to say. There were a few older people carrying antinuke signs, but they seemed overcome by the weight, and one by one they dropped exhausted into the shade. The only people he could see displaying any energy at all were gay. Women with grayish hair cut short, men walking in pairs. They stopped near the footbridge to snap off flowers from their stems, adorning themselves with the blossoms. Several carried signs that were larger than the peace signs, more professionally printed, and easier to read. Stamp out AIDS, one read. The people holding them twirled them around in their hands.

By the time they reached the Common there were hundreds of them. Hundreds, then thousands. He prided himself on reading what was in a crowd's heart, but their strut, their flamboyance, their delight in the heat, only confused him, and he wasn't sorry when the main stream veered right, leaving him to continue on more or less alone. The speaker's stand, mercifully, was set up in the shade of one of the last and tallest of the elms. A few dozen people milled around the amplifiers at its base. As he walked over, he noticed something odd. Grass. Empty grass where always before had stretched a field of brightly colored bandannas, dresses, and shirts.

Jimmy Hoffman was over by the sound truck handing out arm bands to his marshalls. He seemed even more nervous and preoccupied than usual. His squeaky voice soared into octaves he had never reached before — his hands waved furiously. It was a few minutes before he slowed down enough to notice his arrival.

"How's it going, Jimmy?"

"Early yet," Jimmy said, following his eyes. "Lots of time."

"Where are the TV crews?"

Jimmy puckered his cheeks. "Screw them. Anyway, you're speaking last. A bunch of people I never heard of, Lucas, Matilda, then you."

"I count maybe two hundred people."

"Count again. I see millions. Just like in New York."

"That was three years ago."

"So? Count the ghosts."

Jimmy took him by the arm and led him up the stairs to the platform with the protective firmness of a manager leading his fighter to the ring. Most of the speakers were already there, scattered in the seats that had shade. A battle was under way between Jack Markowitz and Ida Brown, the rally organizers. The Quakers hadn't been called; the women's groups were busy elsewhere; it was the wrong day to choose. They went at it with every ounce of their organizational passion, flailing each other's shoulders with the rolled butts of their programs. Jack's face had turned flabby since the last time he had seen him. Ida's breasts, one of the delights of the Sixties, sagged to her waist.

He had just settled into his chair when a hand shot out and slapped him on the back.

"Oh, what a glorious afternoon!" Lucas bellowed, in his best Southern Baptist style. Several people applauded, startled by his voice into thinking the rally had begun.

"Oh, it's a fine afternoon. I'm talking a *fine* afternoon. We're going to twist that Pentagon tail some today, eh Thomas? Going to make those folks in Washington sit up and take notice. Take notice *now!*"

"Impressed by our numbers, they will surely succumb."

It was Matilda who said it. Opposite as they were, she always dogged Lucas's shadow that way, making it seem as if his optimism carried its own shadow. She was half his size, wrapped as usual in the heavy shawls that hung down her body with the delicacy of chain mail.

"Can't you see it?" she said, settling into the chair next to him. "The cabinet resigns, the navy is scuttled, all our missiles are converted into toaster ovens, and the world is saved. Hello, Thomas," she said, sticking out a bony hand. "Long time no see."

"You're looking great, Matilda. What is it, forty pounds? Very impressive."

She took out a cigar, one of her small ones. "Liquid diet. I absorb two hundred and fifty calories a day, not counting gin. You're looking pretty good yourself. Charles Boyer. Older, but with grace. How's Christina?"

"Christina is fine. We keep in touch. She's having a baby."

He waited a decent interval, then pointed to the grass. "This is a seminar, not a rally. Where are they all?"

"Oh, beautiful crowd!" Lucas said, squinting into the sun. "We're talking fifty, sixty thou at least. Dust off your elocutionary talents, Father Tom. These are folks waiting to be *moved!*"

Lucas's blindness could be refreshing at times, but given the humidity, he preferred Matilda's realism. It was good for his staleness. Her voice had a gritty quality that was just what was needed to scrub it away.

"Trends and styles, Thomas. One year peace is fashionable, the next year it's not. TV is sick of us. We don't cut it in the ratings, therefore we don't exist. Over there is the real show."

She pointed toward the other side of the Common. There was a huge crowd fanning inward from the street, pennants and posters waving overhead like the banners of a crusading army set to march. There was music, a swelling roar. Helicopters swung back and forth over the thickest concentration — trucks with cameras circled its perimeter. A balloon broke loose, then hundreds, welling up toward the sky in a dazzling silver cloud.

"There's your true cause for the times," Matilda said. "Sexual repression, with a touch of pathos to make it play. Down with all fleshly ills, down with remorse and mortality, down with AIDS. How vague and ungraspable is the doom we're preaching when compared to that."

He shrugged. "It's too hot. Peace goes better in the spring. Simple as that."

She looked at him with an earnestness he had never seen in her before. "What we need is a messiah," she said.

"We already had one."

"A messiah," she said, jabbing her cigar toward him. "It's

what it's going to take. A new messiah, and you're the only candidate in sight."

"Starting up now!" Lucas yelled. A young priest and a young nun were reading the invocation in unison. "Brothers and sisters," they began, but their voices were too timid to rise above the distant shouts.

They mumbled on for a few more minutes, then Sandy Fenton got up with his banjo to sing one of his songs. Old Sandy, whose voice cracked on the high notes now, worn thin on every good cause since 1938. Old Sandy, who kept stealing envious glances at the AIDS mob, and who was probably making up a song to flatter them even as he sang.

The speakers started after that. Robert Cormier from Physicians for Social Responsibility talking about the dangers of the MX. Stacy Peters from the United Action Committee talking about peace camps in Britain. Betsy Connors McGill from Citizens for a Nuclear Free Cambridge talking about nuclear-free zones. Each of them read out an entire speech, making no concessions at all to the lack of a crowd. They thumped the microphone in indignation, paused for cheers, did tricks with their voices, building toward a dramatic finish only to be met with the cricketlike applause of the few dozen who were left.

Lucas did his soul-suffering act, then Matilda came on, speaking sensibly as always, turning boldly to face the distant AIDS demonstration, whereas everyone else had pretended it wasn't there. His turn was coming next. He looked at his watch. One twenty-five. Only now did it occur to him that he had nothing prepared. There was his standard speech, but they had all heard it a hundred times, and most of its effects were rhetorical and depended on having a sizable crowd to answer back.

He turned sideways in his seat to gain more shade, hoping the coolness would jog his thoughts. His mouth tasted bitter. He signaled for some water, but Jimmy was busy shepherding around the one lonely reporter to show up. The heat was unbearable now. He thought again of ordering everyone to the beach.

"The bad times have come for us," Matilda was saying. "We in the peace movement must be content to act as irritants until the good times return."

He wiped his hand across his forehead, straining to find the right phrase. My dear friends, he began. My dear friends. Always before he had started that way, and the simple words simply said would act as a catapult. My dear friends, then a sermon. My dear friends, then a speech. My dear friends, but this time there was nothing. No pity to launch in exuberance, no eloquence to propel it, nothing inside him except fatigue and reluctance and doom.

"My dear friends," he said, slapping his hands. "My dear friends."

He got abruptly to his feet. Matilda was having trouble with the mike, and in the confusion caused by the readjustment he made his escape. No one noticed him leaving. He was down the steps to the grass by the time Matilda started speaking again. Jimmy was over by the loudspeakers. He grabbed him by the arm and tugged him behind the stand.

"Can I borrow your car?" he said, making it more a demand than a request. Now that his decision had been made, he was impatient and it was all he could do not to tear the keys from Jimmy's pocket.

"Car?" Jimmy said.

"I need to go somewhere."

"What about the speech?"

"I wouldn't run out without a good reason, you know that, Jimmy. It's something bigger than I happen to be right now."

Jimmy acted reluctant; he looked over his shoulder for help, but in the end he handed over the keys. "It's on Charles Street," he said. "First hydrant, if the bastards haven't towed it. Yellow Escort with dents."

"Thanks. I'll fill it with gas."

"Hey, you don't like talking to ghosts?"

But by then he was gone, walking away from the platform, away from the speeches, away from the AIDS crowd that behind him released their remaining balloons with a loud and defiant cheer.

He didn't own a car, and those rare occasions he drove were all the more welcome for that reason. His delight at being unreachable, the concentration on things mechanical, the separate solitudes of the other cars. All these things acted on him as a balm, and as he sped down the Southeast Expressway past the *Globe* building he waited impatiently for the soothing to begin.

There wasn't much traffic. What cars he saw were rusty dropouts on the great march to the beach. Jimmy's heater was jammed on, and it added a hot stream of air to the blast from the window. Out to his left he could see the bay, but it was the same dull color as the cement. Braintree had three exits. On a hunch, he took the second, spinning down too fast off the exit, nearly skidding. There was a traffic circle at the bottom, and he went around twice before deciding on a road. Two miles, three miles. He passed a string of bars without finding the right one, and was just about to turn around when he saw a flashing neon sign up ahead on the right. Green Parrot, it read. Homemade Muffins and Buns.

He pulled into the parking lot, not quite believing his eyes. It was an old-fashioned kind of diner, long and narrow, its siding a brilliant overlap of red and silver chrome. There was a plaque in front saying that it was on the National Registry of Historic Places, which was appropriate enough. It was a classic — a monument to the times. Spotless food, spotless rest rooms, spotless infidelity.

There were only three other cars parked there, and none of them looked small and expensive enough to belong to someone like her. He leaned toward the mirror to comb his hair, feeling the same juvenile rush of excitement he had felt on the phone. The parking lot was freshly blacktopped. He detoured around the wet spots, trying not to breathe in the creosote smell. For no reason at all, he remembered the summer afternoon thirty years ago when he had taken his vows. He had bought a new blue suit for the occasion. It was the nearest to being a groom he ever thought he'd come.

The sun off the siding blinded him, and it was a few seconds before the diner's interior darkened into focus. It was the real thing, all right. Long marble counter with swivel stools, booths separated by initial-carved partitions, shiny malt machines, a throbbing jukebox. The record that was on was old enough to be vaguely recognizable — it seemed to match the smell of the cooking french fries, to be their song. A waitress came out rump-first through the kitchen door. She switched on a TV mounted above the coffee maker, then limped back toward the grill. The Red Sox game. A truck driver in the last booth looked up at the screen without interrupting his chewing.

There was no sign of Rachel. He walked along the booths to make sure, but there were only five or six people in the place, and most of them had the glazed, hopeless look of the recently deinstitutionalized. A man in a velour hat shuffled six empty coffee cups. A woman in curlers slipped pickles to a miniature collie. A teenager held a comic book upside down. All of them were overdressed for the heat. It made it seem as if they were in a state of suspended animation, waiting for autumn to set them free.

The waitress swept past him again, this time with a tray of dirty plates. "We don't have a hostess or anything," she said, disgusted at his ignorance. "Anywhere you want."

"Someone's joining me."

"Lucky you."

He sat down at the far end of the counter where the light was softest. Above him was an old wooden fan. It spun listlessly back and forth, without the energy to complete a full revolution. The counter itself was even more old-fashioned, with a looping black-and-white grain. There was a Fifties massiveness to it, as if it were meant to support not only elbows, forearms, and heads, but half the total despair in Massachusetts. The section nearest him hadn't been wiped since morning. The smear made him reluctant to put down his arms.

"Yeah?" the waitress said.

"I'll wait."

"You have to order something," she said. She said it sternly, as if she could read the lust in his heart.

"Coffee."

"And?"

He stared bewildered at the menu, helpless as always when faced with a small decision.

"Rice pudding's fresh," the waitress said, tapping her pencil on the marble.

"Rice pudding then."

The door opened behind him. He had decided upon the paternalistic-but-not-too-paternalistic expression that would be appropriate and was halfway toward assuming it, when he realized it wasn't Rachel but a harassed-looking mother with three small kids. They were dressed neatly enough, in bright yellow sunsuits, but there was a jaded look on their faces, as if they were drugged from too much sugar.

"Here you go, mister. Regular's moldy, so this is decaf."

He sipped it slowly, trying to come to terms with the guilt rushing into the vacuum where his desire had been. What had happened when Matilda introduced him? It worried him, and then he realized that in all likelihood nothing had happened. Nothing would happen. War would not come closer, the arms race would not heat up, mankind would move not one millimeter closer to destruction. His leaving would be a forgotten detail in a forgotten rally dismissed in a wire-service report no one would read. And if anyone did question him on it, he could do what everyone else did in similar circumstances. He could issue a statement to the press.

A statement. For a moment, it gave him the same ironic coolness he had experienced that morning when he glanced at the phone, but, if anything, the relief was even more short-lived, and a second later he was sunk back under the humidity's full weight. For what could his statement be about? He tried to compose one in his head, but again, the only part that would come was the start. My dear friends.

He sat there two hours in all. After a while he worked out a truce with the waitress. She filled his coffee cup every fifteen minutes, but no longer bothered him about food. No one else came in the entire time. Those that were already there sat motionless above their plates — nothing broke the silence except the bored drone of the Red Sox announcer up above them on TV. Once the game ended the news came on. It started off with five minutes on the AIDS rally. The full treatment — the balloons, the laughing couples, the out-stretched banners and interlinked arms. He understood now the energy he had marveled at. They weren't protesting a disease but celebrating it — celebrating the fact that their oppression had finally reached a tangible form. Like blacks, like women, they had found their cause. It was no wonder that they sang.

He understood that, and one more thing besides. Rachel would not be coming. Her eagerness on the phone, her teas-ing invitation — they had been whims, made of the same bored stuff as his impulse to call her. And it was odd, but now that she wasn't coming he could picture her in vivid detail. The boyish shortness of her auburn hair, the confi-dence of her face with its deep-set eyes, the slimness of a body that looked totally incapable of ever bearing a child. He could picture these things with the longing of a lover looking back on a bittersweet affair. An ex-lover. And maybe that was what his fifties held in store for him, skip-ping over all the parts of life but the ex- parts, going straight to the regret without the preliminary satisfaction that made it worthwhile.

He had signaled the waitress for his check and was getting up to leave when something strange happened. He noticed a speck on the counter below the wet rim of his saucer. At first, he thought it was a bee, caught there in the sticky net of crumbs. A bee with its body curled into itself ready to sting. He flicked his finger against it to brush it away, but nothing happened. He tried again, his nail snapping down with a little *thwack*. It was only when he swept his hand over it that he realized the bee was inside the marble, safe from his touch.

"Here, look at this!" he yelled, startled.

The waitress came over, indifference set before her eyes like a cloud. "What's matter?" she mumbled. She reached automatically for the coffee.

He pointed. "Look. No, closer this way. Stand over here where the light hits it."

She looked at him as if he had ordered Peking duck — as if he had finally proved weird enough to penetrate her daze. Still, she looked to where he pointed.

"It's a bee," she said, frowning. "What's it doing in there, anyhow?"

"It's a fossil. An animal who lived upwards of five million years ago."

"How'd it get inside there?"

"The marble's a kind of limestone. Limestone is formed by sediments. It probably lived in the sea, and when it died, its skeleton became part of the sand."

"A bee?"

"Well, it's not a bee. It only looks like one. See these little scoop-shaped legs? They must have been used for swimming."

"Yeah?" She touched it gingerly. "What's it called?"

"A Coronus," he said, making it up. "A Coronus Megalothic."

She giggled. It shook the stupor from her face. "Wait until I show Kenny," she said, rushing out to the kitchen. When she came back it was with a squat, hairy-chested man wiping his hands on a gingham apron.

"Look!" she said, pointing.

The chef squinted, then slowly smiled. "Well, I'll be damned!"

"It's a Corona," the waitress said.

She went over to get the truck driver. He had to squint

longer to see it, but was even more excited once he did. The man in the velour hat came over and stood shyly near the stool, getting up on tiptoe so he could see. The woman in curlers held her dog up so he could sniff it. The teenager asked several intelligent questions, then stepped aside so the mother could show each of her kids.

"What's it called?" they demanded, pressing against his legs.

He told them its name and how it had come to be there. "There are probably others in the counter," he said. "The Coronus undoubtedly traveled in schools."

He deployed them out around the counter, assigning each of them a separate section. The waitress thought she spotted one over by the menu holder, but it turned out to be an imperfection in the marble's grain. The truck driver thought he found one, too, but it was only a chip. The little girl found six, but they were all smeared-on bits of food, and no one had the heart to disillusion her. They covered the entire counter inch by inch, bent their heads over the surface like prospectors, swept the grime off with napkins, but no one found any, and it wasn't long before they got bored. A few more minutes and they were sitting back in their booths with the same slack look as before.

"Hey, mister!" the chef said. "This Corona worth anything?"

When he told him it wasn't, the chef scowled and yelled at the waitress for interrupting him. The waitress cursed him back. Someone turned the jukebox louder. The fan groggily spun.

He ordered more coffee. He rubbed his hand over the counter, unable to find the energy to get off his stool. He felt rooted there, screwed in place. "My dear friends," he mumbled, his tongue thick from the coffee's acid. "My dear friends."

My dear friends. The extinct Coronus in its day was the most marvelous creature in a marvel-filled world. Dwelling in the sea as it did, it was not content with mere drifting, but developed specialized means of locomotion, the better to swim toward the warmth of the Pleistocene sun. By its craft and intelligence it soon established dominion over all the other rudimentary life-forms then extant. It was a dominance tinged with mercy, for never did Coronus forget its origins in the common primeval slime. It lent humility to its manners, modesty to its ambitions, and for aeons kept its love of warmth and light within bounds. Generations of Coronus copulated, gave birth, and died, their slender husks sinking to form a layer on the ocean floor that — decaying — nourished new life in return. There was glory in the flow of it. There was beauty in Coronus's heart, an energy that enabled each individual to reflect a fragment of sunlight that in the mass formed an overpowering shine.

And then came the day Coronus left the sea. A little skip at first, then a longer glide, then the steady evolution of wings. For Coronus had within its beauty a fatal flaw. Whatever was evil and dangerous was mistaken for what was desirable and good. The ancient customs were abandoned as useless. The sky that harbored marauding seabirds came to seem the very threshold of paradise. Coronus left the sea to become airy morsels of protein down great hooded beaks. As its numbers declined, Coronus became indifferent to its fate, and when it became indifferent to its fate it was doomed. Mating was less frequent; the single Coronus became the norm. The knack of mirroring sunlight was gradually lost to it — its chevroned flight deteriorated into a random buzz. It turned on itself, becoming cannibal. It sank back again into the ancestral ocean, its wings absorbing the water that had once buoyed its hope. Soon Coronus perished. Soon all that was left were crumbs.

Crumbs. He reached his arm out to brush them away, his arm that felt leaden and lifeless, an appendage of his despair. In moving sideways, it knocked against the coffee, spilling some over the cup's edge. The stain spread down the counter, covering the embedded fossil then uncovering it again, the light playing off the wetness in such a way that the fossil winked.

A friendly wink, he decided. A wink of brotherhood. The wink of kin.

Brooklyn Wept

I'M SORRY, Brooklyn.

All you out there in Bushwick, the good folks of Flatbush. Hey, I apologize. I apologize to my friends at the 81st Precinct listening to the game via radio, all the colored kids pressed in front of the TV window at Abraham and Straus, the butchers there on Nostrand Avenue who sent me the salami on my birthday last July. Apologies to Blanche Thomasina knitting socks in the right-field boxes, crocodile tears streaming down her face like Niagara Falls. To little Jackie Fifer in his wheelchair back of the dugout. To the Dodger Symphonette tootling away out there in the bleachers, something dirgelike, something blue. Apologies to the gamblers that had us at six to five. Apologies to Mayor Wagner and Senator Keating and all the other dignitaries that saw fit to come, and of course to Mr. Rickey, who gave me my start. I apologize to one and all for blowing the Series like that. But to set the record straight on just one factor. It wasn't my fault. It was because Sammy Sampinosa throws like a girl.

Like a girl. A female thrower. A dame. D-A-M-E. Sampinosa. Yes he does.

So okay, faint. Swallow pencils, express varieties of shock. Larry "Larrapin" Poronto, pride of the Dodgers, team captain for thirteen big seasons not counting the war (*Enterprise*, Navy Cross, commissioned from the ranks) is blaming the error on poor Sampinosa, who's lucky to pull in seven grand a year. Course the scorer didn't see it that way, neither did you gentlemen of the press corps, radio correspondents, TV interviewers, wire-service stringers, and assorted hangers-on. LARRY'S LAPSE, PORONTO'S PAUSE — I can see the headlines now. Dust off that old VE-Day type, boys. This is news.

You hear me back there, Bernie? I see your sniffly green nose, so the rest of you must be lurking around behind it somewhere. Why not step out and ask me questions like a man? Pretend you're something you're not. I mean, this must be a juicy moment for you. All those columns about how Poronto's a has-been, and now it's true. Or semi-true. You're book smart and street smart and not bad with words, but you wouldn't know true glory if it kissed you on your private area. See this? Right above my head here? A halo, Bernie. I'm in heaven. I'm angelfied.

Of course I blew it. Eight thousand per man winner's share down the drain-o, ditto the endorsements, ditto the fame. I'll tell you guys the whole story, but first you've got to promise me one thing. The moment Mona shows up, I want all this horse manure to stop. No pictures, no questions, no nothing. I know some of you think otherwise, but she's a sensitive girl down inside, so go easy, okay? And for crying out loud, get those clams to cover up. I mean, what am I supposed to say? Hi hon, these are the guys. That one over there with the botched circumcision is our left fielder Shamsky; the guy with the stiff one is Ike Skoby, pitches in relief; the guy without any is Big Bobby Morgan, and yeah we can't figure out where it went either. Cover 'em up!

Okay, here goes. On the record, every syllable. I, Larry "Larrapin" Poronto, pride of the Dodgers, team captain for thirteen big seasons not counting the war (Mona Treeshime of Honolulu, bar girl or pretty close, whirlwind courtship, married in six sweet days), blew the World Series thereby breaking a borough's heart on account of Sammy Sampinosa throws like a girl. Plus miscellaneous distractions.

It started back there in March. We're playing the Cardinals in Ft. L'Dale. Charlie always let me take my time breaking in, but it was a nice day so I figured what the hell. Bottom of the second Musial leads off. Bummer fools him with a spitter he just manages to tip off toward third. Sampinosa scurries after it, comes up throwing. Like I had maybe a million times before, I glide over to the bag. I'm standing there in the kind of warm, springtime glow you get in when your muscles are rounding into shape, waiting for the ball to smack against the pocket of my glove, when I feel a cramp in my leg back of the knee. A sort of spasm. A shivery kind of spasm that seemed to ripple up my spine to my head into my eyes.

That was the funny part. The way the sense of feel and the sense of sight came together like that, the one twisted around the other making each more intense. Any of you guys know anatomy? The legs and eyes are separate organs, aren't they? Somehow they got tangled. The worse my leg hurt, the sharper my eyes seemed to focus. All the years me and Sammy played together, all the times I'd taken his throws, and this was the first time I ever noticed his follow-through, actually noticed it as a separate motion. Instead of flicking his arm diagonally across his chest like this, he let it collapse straight overhand like this. Nope, like this. Limp. Like a girl at a summer softball game who puts everything she has into her throw, all her muscles and sexiness and child-rearing capabilities, then immediately lets her arm go slack like she's denying the effort she's just made. A girl throwing like she means it, then standing there like she doesn't. It's beautiful and feminine and seeing it in a buffalo like Sampinosa caught me by surprise. By the time I recovered, the ball's sailing past me and I have to pirouette to my left to make the play. A second later I'm hobbling around the infield grass trying to work the kink out of my leg, trying not to let anyone see me smile. Sampinosa threw like a girl!

"You okay, Larry? Larry, you okay?" Charlie waltzes around me like a sheepdog ready to write off the whole season then and there.

"Yeah, just a cramp no sweat."

He cups his hands over his mouth, screams over toward third. "Come on, Sammy! Get in the game! Straighten them out for crissake!"

And that was it. I don't think two people in the whole ballpark noticed. Three counting you, Bernie. I glanced up at the pressbox and saw the sun glint off your glasses, and not only them but your binoculars and not only them but your lousy Smith-Corona. Before the next pitch you had it all down. How Larry "Larrapin" Poronto, pride of the Dodgers, team captain for thirteen big seasons not counting the war ("the draft dodger," "the cushy assignment," "the phony sailor of the East"), was over the hill. Over the hill, down the far slope, halfway underground. The man who some claim was the slickest-fielding first-sacker in baseball

history put on an exhibition of tangle-footed artistry this
P.M., leading observers to question whether his weary
thirty-nine-year-old body is up to the rigors of another cam-
paign. Poronto, notorious for his off-season high jinks amid
the Midtown fleshpots, is obviously beginning to show signs
of wear and tear.

I read it that night in the bathtub. I'm usually a fast
shower man, wipe the armpits, rinse the dong, and I'm done.
But my leg was hurting, I felt like relaxing, so I sat there
like the *Queen Mary*, happy as a seal. Mona was fixing her
makeup in the mirror. I tried explaining about Sampinosa,
but she wasn't interested.

"Bernie is right," she said. "You are getting old. You
haven't cheated on me in at least a week now. Not that I
know of anyhow."

That's how she talks — mock-tough. You'll see for yourselves when she gets here. She had her brassiere all adjusted,
and she was pulling her dress over her head, smoothing it
down.

"Where you going?" I said. I leaned forward to massage
my leg.

"None of your beeswax."

"I thought maybe you'd stay in tonight, seeing how we're
going north soon."

She took her eyes off the mirror long enough to stare
down at me. Say this for Mona. When she stares at you,
you know you've been stared at. It's those Hawaiian eyes of
hers. Cannibal eyes like a cat's. They make you horny and
scared at the same time.

"I'm going out," she said, shifting the gum to the other
side of her mouth. "Where I am going and who I am going
with is none of your concern."

"I just wondered."

"Yeah, well let me tell you something, slugger. I just wonder, too. I just wonder for nine years now. A blonde this time, or is it a redhead? I can't keep score."

The water was getting cold, so I let in some hot. "I do my best," I said.

She started out the door. It was funny, but seeing her go I felt a hollow spot in my gut. "Mona?" I yelled.

She clapped her hands over her ears.

"Your hair looks cute that way!"

That really startled her. She reached up and patted it like she was checking it was still there. "I always wear it like this," she mumbled.

"It's cute. I never noticed before."

Just for a second, just for a split second she tilted her head a bit to the side, looking at me the curious way she used to when we were first married and I got MVP honors. "Honey?" she said, real husky-like.

"Yes, Mon?"

"Don't drown. I wouldn't want to lose a Series share this early in the season." With that she slammed the door.

See what I mean about her sense of humor? And that was pretty smart of her, too, thinking we had a shot at Series dough when all you scribes picked us for last. We started lousy, but by May we were rolling along on that eight-straight tear. Shamsky was hitting like a son of a bitch, Bummer had his spitter under control, and Morgan was leading the league in six different categories, not counting shortest dong.

What was it, thirteen, fourteen straight before we dropped one to Cincinnati? I'm leading off from first bottom of the ninth two out tying run at third, Shamsky up with a chance to win it all. I look over to Pig Pitler in the coaching box for the sign, take a few steps more still playing it safe. Damn if it doesn't happen again. The cramp. Right from my leg up to my eyes. I look back at Pig, I see him in a totally different light. He wasn't flashing signs, he was dancing. Touch of the nose, touch of the elbows, pat of the rump, wiggle of hips, shake of the leg — cha, cha, cha. Like a deaf person dancing in Hula language, languid and sexy. I'm looking over at him laughing out loud really enjoying it, I hear a sudden roar from the stands, I hop back quick but too late — I'm picked off first by three feet.

Mona! Hey, Mona! Over here, baby! No? Well, tell me when she does, okay? Keep a space clear and everything. I want you photogs to catch the expression on her face when I hug her. From the right. Her left cheek's got a beauty spot on it which I'm nuts over, but she's a little self-conscious, know what I mean?

So everyone was a little pissed at me for breaking the string, but no one said anything. Except you, Bernie. Is it because you blame me or what? Because we're the same age and your fingers don't fly over the typewriter keys as fast as they used to? I'd really like to know, because there it was in the *Tribune* the next day about how middle age is a terrible thing. The truth of this statement is painfully obvious to anyone who watched Larry "Larrapin" Poronto ("the wencher," "the boozer," "the discredit to the game") doze off yesterday afternoon in the cozy vicinity of Ebbetts Field's first-base bag. A man reaches forty, his heart starts to go. The intensity wears thin, the instincts rebel, the sharp hungry want in the gut becomes sated and slack. The Dodger management would do well to install a rocking chair in the dugout for Old Man Poronto, the better to rest his arthritic bones. With Poronto on first, der Bums are doomed.

Which shows you what kind of prognosticator Bernie is. We were flying. Gabby threw his back-to-back no-hitters, we won four straight from the Giants at home, went over to the Polo Grounds and swept four more. By August we were what? Eight games in front? Brooklyn went nuts, you couldn't buy a seat for love or money.

Meanwhile, I was noticing more and more. The way the infield grass smelled when we first went out there in the morning, the echo of the P.A. announcer's voice as it got lost in the right-field corner, the way the sky looked up there over the bleachers when it got to late innings. I mean, the smells and sights and sounds must have been there all along, but I was running too fast to see. With my leg going bad, it slowed the blur down just enough so I could pay attention. Understand? You're a kid, you're in the middle of everything, life is this big fast vanilla swirl, what do you see? Nothing. You're part of the frosting. Get to forty, you're more towards the cone.

The fans, for instance. Here I always thought of them as a bunch of lazy Romans sitting there in the amphitheater watching us toreadors box it out. Now though, I started paying attention to their faces. I mean, it surprised me that they even *had* faces. I'd drift over to the rail for a pop-up, and while I was waiting for it to come down I'd take my eyes off the ball just long enough to peek at whoever was sitting there in the boxes. The variety was amazing. Old guys in dapper straw hats, young GI's with dates, kids in Dodger caps wearing their hope up front in their eyes. Amazing. Humans! People who breathed, burped, and laughed.

I remember one time there in August trying to explain all this to Shamsky. It was the night he passed Mays for the league lead in homers, so we went out to celebrate at this place in the Village where you press guys wouldn't bother us. Shamsky's got this bulky all-American body beneath a pretty sharp Jewish mind, so I figured he was just the man to talk to.

"There's this old lady with a quilt over her legs sitting behind the dugout. She must have been ninety, ninety-one. There's the ball falling right down on her noggin, and what does she do? She winks at me! Goddam winks! 'God bless you, Mr. Poronto.' She says it soft like she's praying. I damn near bobbled it."

Shamsky nodded, stared over at the bar at these two blondes kicking their legs back and forth in our direction.

"Come on, Shammy. I'm trying to explain."

"Over there is the only kind of explanation I need, Lawrence. Two of them. Forty-inch explanations, one for each hand."

Shamsky can be pretty crude when he's not hitting homers. I tried again, but his mind was on one thing.

"And what is wrong with that may I ask?" he said, all offended. "There was a time when you would be over there faster than I. What the hell are we waiting for?"

"They're hookers."

"When did this ever stop you?"

"Mona," I began.

Shamsky wouldn't let me finish. "Mona? You want to talk about Mona? I saw her last night, you know that? I saw her at the Copacabana and she was not alone either."

It's funny, but I felt my heart skip a beat, really skip one. "Who was she with?"

"A guy."

"Knock it off. Who?"

"Someone you know."

"On the team?"

"Aw come on, Larry. Let us have some fun. They are

Dodger fans, I can tell by the way their knockers point. I did not hit three roundtrippers today just to sleep alone."

"I'm not in the mood."

"Poronto is not in the mood! Since when? You are in love or something?"

"Mona and I are doing all right. I see things in her. She has a lot of hidden qualities."

Shamsky looked dubious. "Hidden is right."

"Which is what I want to talk to you about. I'm seeing things, Shammy. Great things. Things I never thought about before."

"You want the one in purple or pink?"

"Like for instance the way you hit those homers."

Shamsky waved the girls over. "Yeah, yeah. Cut the comedy."

"I never stopped to think about it before, but you have the classic swing. They talk about Williams and DiMag, but you're even smoother. More natural. Compared to you, Williams swings like an ax murderer with rusty hinges."

I was getting excited now. I talked even louder so everyone in the joint could hear. "It's not even a bat you're swinging. It's like a scythe. You swing like a peasant who's been out there in the fields scything away for years and years. Centuries even. It's in your blood. You're the eternal scyther."

Which was true, but I probably shouldn't have told him. It made him self-conscious, tied him up in knots. What was it, September before he hit another one? Shamsky's a natural force on the order of a tornado, and here I had him thinking about peasants and scythes and all. By Labor Day our lead was down to two and a half, and Bernie was twisting the screws about how Larry "Larrapin" Poronto, has-been first-sacker of the slumping Dodgers, found a new way to commit an error last night, this one costing the Bums another game. Poronto, reaching up for what should have been the game-ending out, suddenly stopped and pointed at something with his glove as the ball flew by. Was it a bird, a plane, or Superman? Those readers who pick *A* are correct. A bird — a brown-and-white street pigeon, Flatbush variety. Mr. Poronto, for reasons known only to himself, has taken to bird-watching in Ebbetts Field.

"He's full of oatmeal," I told Mona that night. She was in the bedroom so I had to shout. "It wasn't a pigeon, it was a bluebird. Who would expect to see one this time of year?"

I was cooking a late supper — steak, wine, the works. I had it all set, I was lighting the candles, when in she came with her pocketbook, a coat on over her dress. She plucked an olive from off the salad, popped it in her mouth, headed straight for the door.

"Hey, Mona?"

"See you later."

"Where you going?"

"Aren't you getting sick of asking that? I'm going out, slugger. I'm going out in a further attempt to salvage something from the shambles of my inner life."

That hurt. "Please don't, Mon. Hey, look. Have a bite first, we'll talk things over. Remember that time I cooked dinner for you when we first met back there in Honolulu? The way the ocean looked through the screens? It'll be just the same. Just like old times again."

She made a face. She spit the olive out onto the carpet. "Eat shit."

Remember, we're talking about a lot of energy. A helluva lot of energy. You'll sense it for yourselves once she arrives.

"Please, Mon. I'm begging."

"I've got a date."

"With that same guy?"

"He's not a guy, he's a gentleman. He's smart, he's funny, and he's got a good job. Besides which, he appreciates me. See this ring? It was his mother's. He gives me stuff all the time."

And it was funny, but only then did something dawn on me. Here I was feeling jealous and all, feeling like there was this giant hand shoving my heart down into my gut like a piston, and all those years I was screwing around with other women, Mona must have felt the same way. The times I came home late, the times I didn't come home at all. I might as well have been jumping up and down on her heart with my spikes. Maybe this should have dawned on me a lot sooner, but at least it was a start, right?

"I'll get you a ring," I told her.

"What kind of ring?"

"A Series ring. The kind money can't buy."

She hesitated by the door. "You guys will never win it. Bummer hasn't pitched a complete game since August. Morgan's in a slump."

"We'll win it."

"How's your leg doing?"

"Lousy, but it'll hold."

"Yeah?" She looked me up and down like I was a horse she was buying. "What would a Series share be this year anyhow?"

"Depends. We play the Yanks, eight thousand at least."

I could see her thinking it over. "This guy I'm seeing doesn't make all that much," she said. "He's talented, but there's no Series share or nothing. In his line of work that is."

There was a minute when I thought she was going to leave, then she shrugged her coat back off her shoulders.

"I'll stay, Larry. You win the Series, I'll stay. But I'm only doing it for the money, understand? You're still the biggest shit I ever met."

That really put the pressure on. More errors in bad spots, average down to .256, a few bonehead moves running the bases. If Charlie had anyone to replace me with, I would have been riding the bench. In a way, I would have enjoyed that. You get a better view of things from the bench. At the plate it was tough. I'd be batting against that kid pitcher the Cubbies have, Marimba or whoever, trying to concentrate, and all I could focus on was how gracefully he kicked his leg up in the air before he delivered. A Rockette kick like Maria Tallchief's. I'd strike out, head back to the dugout with my head hanging, trying not to let anyone see me smile. But it was beautiful the way he threw. The way the flags streamed in the wind up over the bleachers, the part left in the grass by a backspinning grounder, the quilt of color formed by ten thousand different shirts back of home. They were beautiful.

Even Bummer's spitter. A lot of batters tick his pitches off, so I'm supposed to hug the line, but instead I'd shade to my right to get a better perspective on his delivery. What I really enjoyed was the way he spat tobacco as he let the ball go. It shot up in a rainbow like the Fountain of Youth. I missed a few shading that way, but I couldn't help it.

"Play 'em right!" Bummer would growl.

I'd trot over to the mound, try to calm him down. "Sorry about that, Bum. It was the clouds."

"The what?"

"Those great big cumulus. They formed a frame around your back as you delivered. You ever see clouds that fleecy? Maybe back in Iowa, but here in Brooklyn? You gotta be awed."

I was awed. Awed and elevated. It was like there were these little jets of air under my spikes raising me above everyone else on the field until I got a bird's-eye view like from a blimp. Off the field, too. I'd stand in the shadows back of the ticket booths before a game, studying the fans on their way in. The pops taking their kids by the hand, tugging them away from the hot dog vendors. The teenagers with their ducktail haircuts, Dodger jackets, pointy black shoes. The old-timers that had probably seen every home game for fifty years. Priests and nuns taking the day off. Watching them I felt like I was part of Brooklyn, riding with its hope and joy, rooting from some nutty, unshakable loyalty deep down inside. It was a beautiful feeling to be part of. I had my ear tilted against the borough's heart.

The night we clinched the pennant I took Mona out to Gage and Tollner's for the biggest lobster money could buy. All the waiters came over to wish me luck against the Yanks, people were sending over menus for autographs, buying us drinks. Mona had on that strapless blue dress she wears when she wants to make an impression, and it damn near blinded me she looked so good.

"How sweet it is," I said, lighting up a stogie.

She smiled. She reached over and took my hand. "Larry, I'm a bit worried about one thing."

"There's nothing to worry about. You never looked prettier."

"Your leg. It's not going to slow you down, is it? We need you on base when Shamsky gets up."

I'd gone down to the travel bureau and booked us two tickets for France leaving the day after the Series was over. It cost plenty, but I figured it would be a good way to get this smart and funny whoever guy out of her system. I was waiting for the right moment to tell her, but she wouldn't let me get a word in edgewise.

"Eight thousand, Larry. Just think. I can buy that sable coat they have in Bloomingdale's. We can go out to Vegas together."

Beaming, smiling like that. She looked like a kid, the sexy, tough-but-not-too-tough kid I'd met there on Waikiki Beach back in '44. I draped my sport coat over her shoulders so she wouldn't get cold, leaned over, and gave her a little bite right there on the earlobe.

"Ummh," she whispered. It was all I could do to sit back down.

"Larry?" she said.

"Another lobster? Sure, why not. This meal is on the Yanks."

"You'll concentrate, won't you? You won't try to watch any blue jays or anything? Bernie says you're a full three steps slower than you were in your prime."

"When did he say that?"

For a moment she looked confused. "Uh, it was in the paper."

"I didn't see it."

"The early editions." She leaned over the table, kind of accidentally on purpose ran her finger along the top of her breasts. "You will hustle, won't you, Larry? Hustle just for me?"

"Don't worry about a thing, sweetheart. This Series is in the bag."

I leaned over and kissed her. "I love you, Mona," I whispered. "Love you more than anything." We went home, it was like old times only better.

She was there with the wives back of third for the first

game. I gave her a little wave leading off — some of you may have wondered who it was for. The first pitch from Ford I take to left, and it gets past Mantle to the wall. I come all the way around and score. The fans went nuts. They stayed nuts, too, right through the first six games. Bummer shut them out that first one, the Yanks took the second on Berra's two home runs, and we split the next four, which brought us all even into today's contest.

It was the best six games I ever had in my life. I was batting what? .440 something? Fielding, too. I was vacuum cleaning balls out of the dirt like a steam shovel. My leg hurt even worse than it did before, but I forced myself to ignore it. I forced myself to ignore a lot of things. The sound of the crowd swelling up like a wave on a long fly ball, then crashing *frump* when the outfielder caught it. The smell of burning leaves drifting in from way off in the suburbs somewhere, reminding me it was October. The desperate yearning Mantle put into his swing when he got a pitch inside. I let the beauty fly on by. It was hard — I felt like I had blinkers over my eyes choking off all that was best in me — but at least I was hitting the ball, back in the same blind rush I had played in as a kid. With each new hit Mona stood up and blew me a kiss. The fans picked up on it, and after a while forty thousand men, women, boys, and girls were blowing me kisses, too, giving me their hearts.

This morning we were out here early for extra batting practice. We finish, Charlie calls us into the clubhouse, has us all sit down.

"Okay, guys. You're pros, I don't have to tell you what's on the line. Eight thousand a man winner's share, a ring you can someday pawn when your luck is down, all the women you can handle. I want you to give it all you've got, a hundred percent, I can't ask for more. Watch Pig for the signs, lay off Ford's first pitch, and play Mantle deep. I want you to remember Mr. Rickey and all he's done for us, and I want you to consider how many poor people there are in Brooklyn who ain't never won nothing in their downtrodden lives and how they're rooting for you all the way."

While he was saying this, he was juggling a ball from hand to hand, and then suddenly he tosses it not to Bummer, who would have been pitching on two days' rest, but to Ike Skoby, who had been strictly in relief.

"Win it for Brooklyn, kid." We damn near bawled.

At first it looked like a bonehead move, with Skoby walking the first three men like that. I bail him out with a diving catch, he settles down. Fastballs, a pretty good curve. By the sixth the Yanks still haven't got a hit, and everyone's starting to sense the kid might just pull it off. Maybe not a no-hitter, but at least a shutout, and that's what it would take because Ford's slider had us muttering to ourselves all the way through. Until Shamsky's homer. It nearly brought the fans out onto the field, and the security guards formed a human chain of steel to hold them back. We were one up going into the eighth. Skoby, rearing back now, strikes out the side.

You could see him shaking a bit between innings, trying to stay calm. Me, it was even worse. I could sense all the hope riding on each pitch, the tense excitement of the crowd, you guys up there in the press box hunched forward with your pencils ready to make us immortal — the *drama* of it all. Here Sampinosa and Shamsky are chattering away totally involved, so deep within the game they didn't even know it. I felt like I was sitting up in the stands chewing popcorn like peppermints, and I had to keep yanking my head back down to field level. "In the game, Larry!" I said, pounding my glove. "In the game!"

Berra leads off the bottom of the ninth. Skoby's nervous; he can see all those big 0's on the scoreboard; he keeps mopping off the sweat. Berra walks on four straight pitches. Collins pops up; one away. Woodling walks. Men on first and second. Charlie goes out to the mound to calm the kid down. He manages to strike out Carey. Two outs. Bauer walks batting for Ford. Bases loaded, up comes McDougal with that funny stance. Sixty thousand fans are on their feet. Skoby peers in for the sign.

"Time out!" I yell.

I walk around pretending I've got something in my eye. The funny thing is I did. A kaleidoscope, right smack in my eye dazzling me with color. I rubbed to make it go away, forced myself to concentrate on the here and now.

"Play ball!"

Skoby winds up. I get set in my crouch, praying McDougal will pull it toward someone else.

Ball one.

"Bear down, kid!" Sammy shouts. "No batter!" Charlie yells from the dugout. "No batter! Easy out now!"

Strike. Out in left field, Shamsky raises his fist.

McDougal takes the next two for balls. Then Skoby does something smart. All game he's been throwing hard stuff, but now he takes something off the ball — McDougal is completely fooled. He sticks out his bat at the last moment and raises a soft pop-up back of first in fair territory.

"I've got it!" I yell, spreading apart my arms. "I've got it!"

Everybody runs. Berra's already crossing home, Woodling's right there behind him, Skoby's coming over to shout directions. It's such a high pop-up only now is it coming down, me right underneath. "I've got it!" I yell again, but the cramps and the seeing are tugging me away, pulling me back so that I'm watching from off in the distance somewhere, my vision expanding until it includes not only the perfect white sphere of the ball, but the October clouds against which it's framed, the lush outfield grass, the high tier of the stands, the thousands of amazed mouths hanging open set to scream, the Stadium itself set like a hatbox in the city spread like a mat on the country like a life raft afloat on the world. I stumble backwards, but my vision is up there in the stars now and there's no coming back. The part of me that's a Dodger still wants to catch it, but the other part of me, the forty-year-old part I could feel being born right there and then, knows it's the last chance I'll ever have to take it all in, to rescue time from the glorious befores and the lousy afters. For a moment everything freezes, then I spin around in a big circle and the world spins with me, spins so fast I'm laughing from sheer joy, roaring in glee, and then I hear a noise like an apple dropping *plunk* from a tree. I see Skoby dive toward me headfirst, his glove extended, but too late. Too late for him, too late for Dodgers, too late for everything. The ball rolls to a stop on the grass.

The Yanks went berserk. Their fans were pouring over the railings to mob them, the cameramen were shoving each other trying to get there first, Shamsky had Skoby in his arms trying to pick him up off the grass, the two of them sobbing like kids. No one paid any attention to the ball. I walked over and picked it up.

The baseball.

It felt softer than I remember it feeling before. The horsehide, the stitches. The seams were raised and it had the commissioner's signature on it in neat black ink. I tossed it from hand to hand trying to get the sense of it back again.

After a while, I turned and lobbed it in a big arc toward the mob where Mona stood. Why? I guess because I wanted her to be part of it somehow. I wanted her to see what I saw.

So that's it. The story you guys are after. Every word on the record, in time for the morning editions. Is that enough for you? Enough to crucify me, Bernie? Bernie? Where the hell is he? I want him around when Mona gets here. Come on. What do you mean a date? What kind of woman would wait for a leper like that?

I told you guys. That's the story. That's it, I'm sorry. I said my apologies, what more do you want? No more commentaries. I already explained.

Mona? I thought it was her. Tell me when she gets here, okay?

You guys. You guys.

I dunno why.

Have it your way. I lost it in the sun.

Mona?

Things to Come:
Maine, 1951

CONCEPTUALLY SPEAKING, Winston Grummer was a long way ahead of 1951. Conceptually speaking, he was up there in the late Fifties somewhere, maybe even a full decade, which would bring him to 1961, which was a whole new ball game, a different era, the second half of the century, which damn near put him out of reach. He was so far ahead of his time he was pure 1991, practically a Twenty-first Centurion — so far ahead of his time he could afford to be sloppy in nonconceptual things like dress, appearance, and transport. So far ahead that the black shiny suit he wore, the wing-tipped shoes, yellow bow tie and rimless glasses, the card-board suitcase he carried, and the 1934 Studebaker he drove weren't the anomalies they seemed but only ballast.

"Ballast," he said, echoing his thoughts the way he did on long drives. "Feet on the ground, camouflage, branch office in the here and now."

He had a hunch even in 2001 he'd be at least five years

ahead of everyone — it was good business being ahead. The ledger book beside him on the seat was thick with new orders, and now and then he would take his eyes off the road long enough to glance down at it in satisfaction, feeling like a farmer whose prize heifer, plump already, is putting on weight.

"Hey fatso," he said, affectionately patting it. "What's for lunch today, hey baby? Who's going to feed us, hey? Who's going to become a rich hick today?"

He was feeling good, there was no denying it. It wasn't just the thick order book or the fact he'd spent the night roughhousing a chambermaid at the last motor court or the way the Studebaker was purring beneath him like a kitten. He was feeling good because he was back on the road again aligned with truth. He was feeling good because he knew what truth was, knew where it was, how to grab it and turn it his way. Good because it was so easy for him now, all he had to do was reach up and close his fist and there it was right there in the center of his palm — truth and riches and the secret of the times.

"Air," he said, shaking his head at the marvel of it. "Pure atmosphere, simple physics, the good old O'Two."

Right there for the taking. Right there for anyone, as long as they could get ahead of their time. He was so far ahead it was wasted in a territory like this one where the roads were gravel and the farms were abandoned and the garages forty miles apart. Still, it was only a matter of time before the ledger book grew so fat it had twins, then triplets, and then there would be so many ledgers sitting there on the front seat the head office would have to buy him a new car to carry them all, wise up and realize how far ahead of everyone he was, find him a territory to match his vision. Time was on his side, so there was no use even worrying about it, and he spent the rest of the morning remembering the shape of the chambermaid's thighs.

"Oh, those sweet potatoes," he said, sighing. "Oh, those baked golden yams."

He stopped only once before lunchtime, a little way in from the state line. There was a picnic area, a bench and a spring. He walked into the woods to take a leak, swung his arms around to get the circulation going, then went back to the car and rummaged through the glove compartment until he found the pliers.

People were a little wary in these parts — it made sense not to shy them. He kept a box of six license plates under the seat, one for each state in his territory, and it was the work of five minutes to make the switch.

"State o'Maine," he said, stepping back to study the effect. They were shiny yet, so he patted some dirt on them and creased back the sides. "Welcome, Winston Grummer, to the State o'Maine."

It paid paying attention to basics. Lots of salesmen didn't pay them any attention at all and wondered why their order books went hungry. Not that he bothered much with other salesmen. He was a loner when it came to that, and he avoided like the plague those motor courts where they congregated for their beer parties and mindless bonhomie. When it came to truth there was more in his hand than in all their sample cases, that was a fact. Those few times he stumbled into one of them, he found himself with nothing to say. He was 1991 and they were 1951 and he couldn't be bothered shouting loud enough to get through.

Still, he could teach them some tricks. The license plates, dirtying up the sheen. Average salesmen spent so much time perfecting their spiels they never bothered trying to understand the wanting, and wanting was what the entire country was about. Geography, too. They stuck to the main roads up the river valleys, taking the path of least resistance, while he drove cross-country across the ridges, getting back into places no one else knew were there. You stirred up things going across the grain like that. You saw a lot everyone missed.

"For instance, birds," he said, puckering his lips. "Hello there, robins. How's the worming, hey? How's the flying weather, hey? When the dead dead robin comes bob bob bobbing along, along!"

He liked anything that was airy and high. The sun, puffy clouds, anything blowing. They focused his attention on the proper medium, kept him in touch with his genius. Back in Bean Town it was already summer, but here spring was only just starting and above the road the branches swayed with the weight of new leaves, gladdening his heart.

"Woops! Road sign! Back her up, Grummer old boy. Clarks Corners Four Miles. Clarks Corners, hey? Lots of Clarks, lots of corners." He glanced at his map, then glanced over at the ledger book, which was crammed full of orders but not so full he couldn't slip in one more. "Clarks Corners," he said, still hesitating, and then from nowhere an apple blossom blew down against the windshield, right down out of sheer air, and he took it for an omen and backed off the two-lane gravel and started up the one-lane dirt.

There was a hill to chug over, but past the crest he was able to coast, and in another mile the trees opened up into the prettiest valley he had seen all day. Meadows, millponds, orchards — a bright dancing river with a red covered bridge. Along it was a scattering of houses, a post office and school. They were white and weathered and sagged in fatigue, but past them, set off by itself near the stream, was an old stable converted into a garage, and he saw to his satisfaction it was the neatest, best-kept building in town.

He drove past it slowly without seeing anyone, turned around and came back again to look things over. The air pump was attached to the side of the garage above a crate of pop bottles. It was an old Whitcomb Standard, judging by the gauge — again, a good sign. He backed up until the bumper was directly beside it, turned the ignition off, got out, stretched like he'd been driving for hours, then with the look of a man casually checking, sauntered around examining each tire in turn.

He stopped when he got to the left rear. He frowned, crouched down so his back was between the hubcap and the garage, then with a smooth, secret motion withdrew a tire gauge from his pocket and applied it to the valve until enough air came out that the tire sagged onto its rim.

He put the gauge back in his shirt, then got slowly back up.

One, he said to himself. Two. Two and a half . . .

"Golly Jesus!" he yelled, shaking his head. "Will you look at that!"

Roger heard the man yell. For that matter, he had heard the Studebaker when it first came past Ike Chapman's place into town, the engine making that characteristic double popping sound as it throttled down toward first. He had good ears for that kind of thing. Good ears in general. It wasn't just that they were acute, but that sounds came to him much sweeter than they came to anyone else. Shrill train whistles that had everyone holding their ears seemed to him purely melodic; rasping buzz saws, up there in the woodlots, were to him the softest of purrs. "Everything's sweet when you're doing something you love," his grandfather used to say, in between shoeing horses and mending carts. "You don't believe me now, boy, but you learn that, you'll be the luckiest man alive."

Well he was lucky. Damn lucky. His face was covered with engine oil, he had spent the last hour and a half on his back under Tom Hale's Chevrolet wrestling a balky water pump, and he was so deep in debt converting his grandfather's stable into a functioning garage he would probably never get out again, but despite it all he was lucky. Business was picking up now, the new house was finished, and Laura was starting to fit in better than when he'd first brought her to town. But even more than these, he was lucky to be doing something he loved, putting parts together, building something, lying there flat on his back beneath a Chevy where the breeze was a gentle one and the chassis muffled everything, even the man's shouts.

"Hey! I said, anybody around?"

Roger finished tightening the bolt, tapped it with the wrench for good luck, then slid the dolly far enough out that he could see toward the bay.

"Tiny?" he said.

There was no answer. Tiny was good help, but rigid about lunchtimes. Roger slid himself all the way out, got up, slammed the hood down, then went over to the sink to rinse his hands. There was a window on that side of the garage, and through it he could see the school yard on the opposite bank of the stream. The grass hadn't been cut yet that spring — there by the swing it was high as a man's waist. Through it, swishing her hands back and forth to clear a path, walked Laura, bringing him his lunch.

The day before, seeing her coming, he had crawled

through the grass like an Indian and grabbed her around the waist, carrying her laughing and kicking across the stream. He was tempted to do it again, but out by the gas pump the man was still shouting, and so he finished drying his hands and contented himself with a last quick look. Laura had come to a stop by the empty swing. She stood there staring down at it, then — putting his lunch box on the seat — pushed it gently back and forth.

"There you are," the man said when he came out. "I was just about to give up."

He was standing by the gas pump — a tall, gangly man with a fedora that was two sizes too big for him and a suit that sagged on his shoulders like a black, furless pelt. His face was jowled, dark, and droopy. He had on glasses, the rimless kind the Japanese officers Roger guarded on Saipan had worn, and there was something in his expression of the same serene self-satisfaction.

"You ever see a May so fine?" he said, turning his palms up like a preacher. "I've been driving all morning and it's gotten finer with each mile. I believe this is the finest little town I've seen in some time. Clarks Corners? Fine name, Clarks Corners. And I see you've got yourself a fine little garage, Mr. . . ."

"Clark."

The man laughed and stuck out his hand. "Winston Grummer, like the prime minister? There's no Grummers Corners, not that I know of . . . Oh, I don't need any gas," he said, as Roger began unhooking the hose. "I'm always careful about that. The minute the gauge gets to half, I fill her right up."

"Check the oil?"

Instead of answering, Grummer turned and pointed toward the Studebaker. It was tilted over on one side like someone had shot it; where the left rear belonged was a pancake of black rubber.

"Tough," Roger said, shaking his head. "Blowout?"

"Leak."

"Tough. Well, help yourself to some air."

Roger waved his hand toward the air pump, then without thinking more about it, turned and walked back in through the bay. He expected to find Laura there waiting for him and was disappointed when she wasn't.

Still, there was no spoiling his good mood. The cars he had finished already, the spring air with its lilac underline, his certainty that things were going to be all right now that winter had passed. Just as he took delight in fitting parts together in an engine, he found delight in having the parts of his life start to mesh. He had seen enough of the outside world to know how hard most people longed to fit in and how few ever did. Here he fit in perfectly, not only with the garage he had started from nothing, the house he had built with his own hands, but with the hills his grandparents had farmed and the woods his father had logged and the sky he had played under as a kid, so that he found pleasure just being there, a physical part of it, and anything else life brought him was extra.

"Excuse me? Hate to interrupt your ablutions, but I'm having some trouble with that air pump contraption thing."

The Grummer man stood there in the doorway smiling bashfully. Roger, who was washing his hands again trying to get them white the way Laura liked, felt a flicker of impatience, but tried not to let it show.

"You crank it up to the right pressure?"

"Forty-four pounds. Yessireebob."

Roger glanced out the window toward the school yard,

shrugged, then followed Grummer back to his car. "She's balky sometimes," he said, applying the chuck. There was a hissing noise — the rubber kicked sideways, then stiffened. Slowly, reluctantly, the Studebaker righted itself back to its full height.

"Well I'll be damned," Grummer said. "Easy as that. Takes an ignoramus like me to make it difficult. Maybe you better put a few pufferoos in those front ones while you're at it."

Roger cursed under his breath, but went around inflating each tire in turn. Grummer kicked the tangles out of the hose trying to help him, then stood there with his thumbs in his lapels like they were suspenders, watching him work.

"You own this place yourself?" he said, shouting to be heard over the air.

"Yes, I do."

"Married? What's your first name again?"

"Roger. Yes, I am."

"Lonely spot for a wife, Roger. Kids, Roger?"

"No."

"Maybe just a squeeze more in that left one for good luck. . . . Well, that's great. A family man who owns his own business. That's great. Small businessmen are the rib cage of this country, Roger. Could you check that back one again? I think some air must have leaked out while we were gabbing."

You're the one who's filled with air, Roger said to himself, but he smiled good-naturedly and did as Grummer asked. If nothing else, it would be a good story to tell Laura at lunchtime. It took all kinds.

"Yes, the small businessman. I envy you, Roger, I really do. Course it's tough being the little man. You can make a living, sure, but when it comes to extras, what do you have?

There's no overtime in your game, no bonuses. Pretty soon those special occasions are slipping by, the wife grows resentful, you start nickel and diming yourself. . . . Before long you're right back to where you started from, dead broke, wondering where the hell it went wrong."

Roger stood up. "Tires are filled, Mr. Grummer."

"It's a tough way to make a buck, running a garage. People always demanding things. Tourists storming in asking stupid questions, dirtying up the john, using your air pump. Using it and blocking off the paying customers so you're losing money every second. Think about it, Roger. Would you give oil away if somebody came in looking for some? Would you give spark plugs away just because someone asked? Of course not. And yet there's one vital ingredient you're giving away daily, Roger, something you just gave away not two seconds ago and it breaks my heart to see it. Do you know what that commodity is, Roger? Do you know what merchandise is slipping away from the fingers of your good right hand even as we talk?"

"What?" Roger said, despite himself.

"Air."

"Air?"

"Right, Roger, absolutely right! Air! That good old O'Two. A vital ingredient in supporting life, but an even more vital ingredient in supporting tires. Take the air away, this nation would deflate to a halt within one quarter of an hour, and yet who's supplying all that air? Mr. Goodyear? Mr. Firestone? Of course not! They're living off the free air given away absolutely gratis by small businessmen much like yourself. Correction. Were living off. Because right here in my trunk I have the machine that's righting the wrong of the century, the machine that's going to reward all your hard labor with some extra cash, the machine that's going to pay you for what's inalienably yours, the machine" — he opened the trunk — "called MAP!"

There where the spare tire ordinarily would have been, lying on a mat of velvet, was a yellow machine the size of a bread box. It was polished with oil and arrogant-looking; there was a huge gauge on the front and a fat coin slot and three red letters in a bold, flowing script.

"MAP?" Roger said, reading them.

"Make Air Pay."

"You're selling air?"

"*You're* selling air."

With that Roger did something he had been tempted to do ever since Grummer began talking. He laughed. He laughed to himself at first, but then it bubbled away from him and got caught up in the ludicrous appearance of the machine and the shabby suit Grummer wore, his huge, out-pointing shoes, the way his jowls flapped, until he couldn't contain himself and doubled over there by the trunk, laughing so hard he nearly cried.

Grummer chuckled himself, as if to let Roger know he wasn't stuffy, then reached in and patted the machine like he was slapping it tenderly awake. "It's a great concept, all right," he said. "Fits right onto your old air pump with three simple bolts. Gives you two minutes of air per quarter. Works out to about a quarter per tire. Average customer comes in for air, you've made yourself a buck. Say twenty people a day, that's twenty bucks . . . times seven . . . a hundred and forty a week. Now I bet there are things you could do with a hundred and forty extra a week, isn't there, Roger?"

Roger looked down at the machine. He had laughed so hard it was all gone from him and he felt impatient and used.

"I don't want it, mister. The answer is no."

Grummer didn't seem shocked so much as hurt. He straightened up with difficulty and began rubbing his back.

"Don't blame you, Roger," he said, after a time. "Don't blame you at all. Lots of people are reluctant when faced with a new idea. Why there was a time when . . ."

He stopped; his eyebrows arched up from behind his glasses and stiffened. "Get a load of that," he said, whistling. "Talk about a nice juicy handful."

"My wife," Roger said.

He left Grummer standing openmouthed by the trunk and walked over to the garage. Laura was already inside by the workbench, looking up at the pinup Tiny had pasted to the wall. He tried tiptoeing up on her, but she heard him, looked around, and blushed.

"Am I as pretty as she is?" she said, in her softest, flirtiest drawl.

He laughed and bent over to kiss her, but she turned her cheek away and her expression, so doll-like, became sad.

"I started today," she said.

"That's too bad."

"I said I started!"

She seemed near tears. Roger wiped his hands on his pants, and held her shoulders this time and kissed her lightly on the cheek.

"Well, we'll try again, that's all. Doctor Richards said it wouldn't be right away. We'll go to another doctor if that's what it takes."

She tightened her lips into a pout. "It's been forever."

"No it hasn't. We'll start again tonight."

"Come home with me now."

It wasn't teasing the way she said it but demanding, and it took him back.

"I'd love to, honey, but I've got work. You know it's been busy here. I'll be home around six and then we'll do something special."

She turned away and mumbled something toward the wall.

"What's that, honey?"

"I can't stand it."

"Can't stand what?"

Instead of answering, she went over to the lunch box and reached inside. "Here, look at this," she said. "I got it in the mail today. It's a flier for this sale they're having at Sears and Roebuck. Right there on the front page. Television sets are only three hundred dollars this week for one week only. We could afford that if we paid on time."

Roger laughed like he had when Grummer mentioned the air. "What's the sense of a television set? There's no reception yet around here. It would just be an ugly box sitting there in the parlor where it doesn't belong."

"Please," she said. "It's the kind I want."

"You know we're saving."

"Please."

This time it was kittenish, and she put her arms around his waist and pulled him in close to her. "It would be nice having a television set, that's all. It would help me when I get blue being all alone."

She kissed him. She kissed him and it was like it always was and the happiness he was so aware of all around became localized deep within him and it was so overwhelming he nearly burst.

"Honey," he whispered, closing his eyes, but just then she jumped back and let out a little shriek and pointed to the window like she'd seen a ghost.

Roger looked. "Oh, Lord . . . Listen. Stay right here. I'll deal with him myself."

Grummer was leaning against his car, lighting a cigarette, trying to act nonchalant, as if he'd been waiting there all along.

"Nice lady," he said. "I didn't mean any offense before."

"Take your machine and get going."

"Sure thing. Let me write up that order first."

"There's no order, mister. Get the hell out of here."

Grummer's jowls puffed toward his eyes like a squirrel's. "Some men would take offense at your tone, Roger. Some men, when they're trying to help a man see truth, would take offense when that help was rejected." He reached up and made a grabbing motion. "That's all it takes. You hear me? All! It's sitting there ripe for the plucking."

"Sell the sun."

"What's that, Roger?"

"You might as well sell the sun. Sell the river over there. Sell the clouds and the wind. Air's free, mister. It's always been free and it's always going to be free and if a sharpster like you can find someone stupid enough to buy it, he can just go and find him somewhere else."

Grummer would have had to be deaf not to catch the warning beneath his tone. He stood there looking down at the machine, talking more to it than to Roger.

"Hey, a nonstarter. Right there stuck in 1951, hey? Man who doesn't want the truth, hey? State o'Maine, hey? State o'Ignorance, hey?" He tilted his head to the side and smiled. "Mr. Clark, I respect you, I certainly do. Here's my card should you ever change your mind. I only hope there are some machines left when you do. . . . Can I ask you one thing? Are there any stores around here? I need a few necessities in the course of my journeyings."

Roger was expecting an argument and it took him by surprise. "Over in Bethel," he said. "There are plenty of stores. Go back out the way you came in."

Grummer took a quick glance at the tires, kicked one affectionately, then got in the front seat.

"Roger," he said, sticking his head out the window. "I wish you a good day. To you and your lovely Mrs., the best of good days."

Roger watched him back up. He watched as the Studebaker disappeared through the covered bridge and curled back down the road past Chapman's, then waited there until the popping sound was gone and the plume of dust had settled. When it was gone — when the scene he loved had dropped back into place — he walked over to the garage.

"Honey?" he began. "You'll never believe . . ."

She wasn't by the workbench. He looked behind the Chevy, but she wasn't there either.

"Honey?"

One May when Laura was little she had sat in the kitchen with her face against the screen door, staring out toward her father, who was weeding in the garden. What she remembered wasn't anything particular about him, but the way the bees danced up and down by his hat, how the roses, so gigantic to her, waved back and forth by his legs, the way the metal strips hung on the clothesline to chase crows flashed in the sunlight, the blur of their wooden goose windmilling in the breeze, the matching click from the robins above the verbena, the way everything smelled of warm earth spiced with cinnamon. She remembered these and how frustrated she had become because there was a thin, prickly screen separating her from it all, making everything a gray, ugly mesh color, and how she had cried at that and how her father, hearing her, came over, opened the door, took her under the arms, and set her down in the middle of the garden so she was content.

She felt that way now — sensed the apple blossoms up there in the meadows and the warmth of the sunlight and the sugar smell of first haying, and yet she was cut off from it by a fine mesh screen, only it was inside herself this time and there was no way through. "Can't you see it?" Roger was always saying, sweeping his arm around indicating everything and nothing at all. She could see it, of course she could see it, warm earth and waving flowers and sweet hay, but she was separate from it now, it wasn't hers.

She felt like that, felt crampy and bloated besides, and she walked quickly past the school, fighting back tears. Recess was out, but she didn't dare look at the children because she knew she would cry if she did. She didn't look toward the post office because Mrs. Brown and Mrs. Hammer were there gossiping and she wouldn't give them the satisfaction of snubbing her. She didn't look toward Mr. Weller's house, because she knew he was at a window somewhere leering at her, wetting his lips. She walked from the garage all the way past Chapman's out of town, and not once did she look anywhere but straight ahead, holding her head high to spite them, not caring what they thought but caring too much about that, so in the end she cried after all, but only when she was past the last house walking alone up the road.

"Think of happy things," Roger was always telling her. "You mope around too much, honey. It's not good for you."

He could be so concerned, so tender, and then the next moment she would tell him she'd started or that the doctor had shook his head, and he would laugh it off or change the subject, and it was just as though he had gotten up and left her alone behind that screen. It was why she wanted a baby in the first place — something so small and so needy it would pull her through to belonging — but Roger couldn't see it and always laughed at their luck and refused to be sad.

She walked along the river road, staying in the middle because it was the only desperate thing she could think of, walking slower the closer she came to their turnoff, wanting something to happen though she wasn't sure what. She had been waiting so long for a baby she had lost the sense of what it was, and the only thing she was aware of anymore was the wanting itself — the cold aching wanting that followed her day after day, so she had no rest from it and it frightened her to be alone.

She walked past the old Bailey place, the curtains blowing out the broken windows, then turned and looked back toward the willows that overhung the road. I'll count to thirty, she told herself. If a car comes, I'll put my thumb out and hitch.

She closed her eyes and counted and for a moment the desperation relaxed her, but then she was up to twenty and there was no sound out there, and then she was slowing down past twenty-eight and still there was nothing, until finally she was at thirty and opened her eyes to the empty road and there was nothing to do then but walk up the hill past the mailbox to their house.

"Hello, house," she said.

It was tucked into the side of the hill where the wind couldn't catch it — a big Cape made from lumber Roger had salvaged from the Bailey barn. It was new and modern and everything she had wanted, but there wasn't much money left after building, so the furniture was secondhand and dilapidated, and she hated it so much she could no longer tell

which was real, the newness of the Cape or the oldness of
the furniture, and whether she should feel proud or
ashamed.

There was one chair in particular. It was round and squat
and shaped like a man's lap and it was covered with a loose,
nicotine-stained chintz that made her want to scrub her
hands after touching it. But it wasn't just the chair, it was
the corroded old silverware they used and the plates with
the cracked edges and their having nothing new except the
house.

"We'll have those things," Roger would say gently whenever she complained. "I bought you a radio, didn't I? That's
the newest radio in town."

The radio. It was new and shiny and crowded with numbers and yet she hated it just as much as the chair, though
it was almost always on. It couldn't see, that was the problem. Radios were fine for just humming to, but they
couldn't make you see like a television was supposed to.
There were times when all her wanting came down to something as simple as that — just to be able to see. See past the
mesh. See past the hills that blocked the views. See past
her flat, hateful stomach to her womb. See past the walls
that were closing in on her to the rest of the world.

She sat down at the kitchen table, then jumped back up
again and went into the bathroom to find some aspirin. She
took six, melting each in turn against the bitter spot at the
base of her tongue. It helped for a time. She felt less crampy
than before and tried her best to cheer up. She swept the
parlor out. She pushed the armchair over toward the drapes
so it wasn't so noticeable. She brought the mirror over and
arranged her hair in different styles. She put the radio on
and started humming. She sat down at the table again and
went through some women's magazines, cutting out recipes

and pictures of babies, filing them in a scrapbook she kept in the cupboard by the stove. For a while, she was able to keep busy, then she ran out of things and it was still only three-thirty and she knew just as she had known since coming indoors what she would do next.

Again, she tried fighting it. She sat down in the loveseat and closed her eyes, trying to block out everything except the music, but it wasn't enough. There in the center of the parlor was a brown hooked rug they had bought at the church rummage sale. The sun, coming through the windows, crisscrossed there and formed a pool of gold when the rest of the room was dark. The brightness was irresistible. The brightness, in the shabbiness, had drawn her there every day that week.

"No," she said. "Not today."

She said it firmly, but walked over to it anyway, then stooped down and took off her shoes. When she got up again she stood very straight facing the window through which the sun poured. She brought her hands up and undid the barrettes until her hair spilled loose, then tossed her head back so it fell down over her shoulders. She waited a moment, facing the window, then slowly unbuttoned her blouse and let it fall to the carpet. She slid her bra around and unfastened the hook and let that fall, too. She pushed her skirt down her legs, stepped out, then tugged the panties down and then her stockings until there was a mound of clothing there by her feet and she stood naked facing the window, her eyes closed, intensely wishing.

She closed her eyes and stood there wishing, her arms motionless at her sides, shivering in the sunlight's warmth, feeling it spread up her legs past the flatness of her stomach along her ribs over her breasts. As warm and soothing as it was, it made her ashamed and she didn't know why she was doing it, but she knew she must stand there naked in precisely that spot if she wasn't to go insane.

She closed her eyes and wished for a baby and then new furniture and then pretty dresses and then for none of those things, until the wishing was there by itself and she stood there naked before it, offering the only thing she had to give, trembling in excitement and fear as the flush spread, and then from the deepest part of her wanting she became aware of a sound, a dry distant popping sound, and then another one, and then it came closer and she realized someone was outside knocking and she caught her breath at the suddenness of it and went dizzy from weakness and only with the greatest difficulty managed to push away from the rug and find her bathrobe and grope past the furniture to the door.

There was no one there. As frightened as she was, she felt nearly crushed from disappointment, but then as she turned to go back inside she saw a box near the stoop. It was a cardboard box, the big kind the supermarkets gave away, and on top of it was a clumsy pink bow.

"Roger?" she said.

No one answered. Down by the road she heard the clanking of gears then saw a yellow car turning left from their driveway. She watched it drive off past the Bailey place, feeling puzzled, then suddenly remembered the box and fell down on her knees beside it and began tearing off the tape and string.

There was a tablecloth inside — a new linen tablecloth with lacy edges, and underneath it was a new serving tray made of what looked to be silver, and beneath that a frilly organza nightgown with ribbonlike straps and beneath that a ladies gold watch and below that a bottle of perfume and below that a neatly folded piece of paper. When she took it out and held it to the light she saw it was the flier with the television set on it and that right in the middle of the screen was a message scribbled in red pen.

"Make Air Pay," the message read. "Call Winston Grummer for fast response."

She looked at the flier, looked into the box with all its treasures, then looked back toward the road and the disappearing Studebaker, and then the flush spread to her cheeks and she brought her hands up to cover them and giggled like a girl.

The Next Sound
You Hear

Dr. WEIRD had mutilated the Bartók for a change. Usually it was the Mozart or Haydn or the other sacrificial albums Silva left exposed on the console to sate Weird's appetite for destruction. This time, though, he had found the good ones hidden away in the back of the studio beneath some old program logs. The Third Piano Concerto — the Deutsche Grammophon version with Anda and von Karajan. When Silva comes on at midnight, already exhausted from a full day of teaching, the album is cued up on the turntable with a glistening X left across the vinyl by the sharp ebony forehead of Weird's skull-and-crossbones ring.

A memo is taped on the mike. It's in red ink, making it seem as though it's been scribbled in some vile pustulation from the ring's maw.

"What is this Hungryian crap, idiot? Do you realize every penny you spend on this albumen goes strait to the Kremlin? Shape up or shit out, pinco. You use the public airways to spew p'ganda like this your going to hear from concerned citizens and i mean the school board in personal. Got that, intellectile? And while i was at it i cleaned up your Doorvack albumens, two. Roll over Baytoven, Dr. Weird."

It's true. When he goes out to the lounge to start some coffee, the Dvořák is spread across the floor like so many crumbs. He stares at them for a long time without moving. They're among the last albums left from his student days in New York — the albums that were the only possessions they had carried with them to New Hampshire fifteen years ago, cradled on Sarah's lap like a pioneer woman's precious china, their sole link to the life they were leaving behind.

The Eighth Symphony. The Stabat Mater. Like crumbs, like trampled crumbs.

He switches on the monitor near the coffee maker so he can keep track of how much time is left on the public-service tapes, then goes off in search of a dustpan and broom. At least Weird hadn't urinated on the pieces the way he had the Stravinsky. When Silva had shown that mess to Berger, the station manager, Berger had only shrugged.

"Don't push me, Silva. I need a caretaker for the weekend midnight-to-dawn spot, and you're the only one in this godforsaken wilderness insane enough to take it. For all intents and purposes, Weird *is* KXP. We were that close to bankruptcy before he showed up, and he's now bringing in seventy-three percent of this station's revenue. You're bringing in zero. End result? I'm prepared to let him have his fun."

His fun. His hard rock and right-wing country. His half-smoked joints left smoldering on the teletype. His pornographic pictures spread across the weather reports. The havoc he wrought with his ring. Silva had saved a few opera albums by hiding them in Johnny Cash sleeves, but even by filling in with the cassettes locked away in the tape cabinet, he only has enough music to program for another two weekends at most.

There's nothing he can do about it now. He plugs in the coffee maker, warming his hands over the steamy lid. As usual, he tries to talk himself into going over to the thermostat and raising it from the forty-five-degree maximum that was all Berger allowed him. As usual, he decides to make do with sweaters. He pours some coffee beans in the hopper, adds some more water, then goes over to the newsroom window to make a visual check on the antenna.

It was on the steep, burned-over mountain back of town. On clear nights in winter the warning lights would become confused with Orion, showing up as ruby ornaments on the buckle of the hunter's belt. Tonight, though, the sparkle is obscured by the white slant of snow, and he has to stare for a long time before making it out. The antenna was said to be the highest object between Montreal and Mount Washington, and in storms like this one it bucked back and forth to improbable angles, doing crazy things to the signal, flailing out Dr. Weird's hostile music, the commercials, the public-service tapes, and the nightly prayer.

"Antenna okay," he writes in the log. "LIKE A GIANT'S DICK," Dr. Weird had written in the space above.

The tape on family violence is just ending, the prayer about to begin. The former is hosted by a reformed child-abuser who speaks with the dulcet, soothing tones of a preacher; the latter is offered by a preacher who speaks with the harsh, violent tones of a child-abuser. Silva lets the sound of it chase him back out to the lounge.

And we promise you Oh Lord to smite down the EEE . . .

VILLL that DWELLS so overwhelmingly in our hearts and I MEAN RIGHT NOW or someone somewhere in some sense is going to be PUNISHED!

Silva sticks his mug under the coffee maker's spout and stirs in some sugar. He has just taken his first swallow — he's slipping the *Butterfly* record from the Johnny Cash sleeve to check the timing — when he suddenly clutches both hands to his throat, runs to the sink, doubles over, and retches.

Tar. It's as if he has swallowed tar spiked with glass. He wedges his head under the faucet gulping in as much coldness as he can, trying to flush away the gumminess that burns his throat. He coughs spasmodically — recovers — coughs again.

"Testing," he says cautiously. "Testing one two three."

It's a while before he gets up the nerve to examine the mug. Floating on top of the brownish coffee is a dark blue pool of something heavier, something that combines the glutinous quality of honey with the metallic sheen of oil. Swarming below it are bits of solid the color and consistency of ground sirloin. He sniffs it, then gags again.

He goes over to check the coffee maker. It looks okay, and it isn't until he picks up the cannister of coffee beans that he realizes what's happened.

Pasted on its side is the memo, the red ink making it all but indistinguishable from the cannister's decorative label. Only the embossed skull and crossbones protrude.

"You like this shit, you may as well drink it, huh tweed-face? Bock on the rocks. A Bock shake. Molten Bock. Eat it raw, eggbrain. I ground the record up in the paper shredder and mixed it in with the coffee, that's how. Just a reminder to stay on your toes. HamBerger is looking for an excuse to can you, dig? Fuck up once and your gone, kulturass. Starting next weekend I want your spot. I want the whole nite cuz the nite belongs to the brave. And dont think about revenge either, your not the type. Pee S. Bock in the stomach cauzes cancer your dead. Roll over Baytoven, Dr. Weird."

The Concerto for Two Violins in D Minor. The one he'd had Nathan Milstein sign eighteen years ago. The album cover shredded atop the coffee beans like white coconut topping.

And since that's the way it is, we'll say AMEN UNTIL NEXT TIME . . . AMEN!

Silva, clearing his throat, hurries back to the console in time to keep the tape from spilling off the spool onto the floor. He sits down on the swivel chair, wipes Weird's hair grease off the earphones, places them on his head, cues up the *Butterfly* ready to play, then changes his mind and reaches under the mutilated Mozart albums for his favorite Beethoven, the *Emperor* with Rudolf Serkin. Once it's ready, he glances up at the clock. For two full minutes he lets the silence re-establish itself — lets the blank hum of the transmitter absorb the echo of the preacher's harsh voice.

"It's to set the mood," he had said when Berger complained. "I need space to mellow things out."

"Mellow smellow. People will think we're off the air. They'll click us off."

And though Silva didn't admit it to Berger, this was precisely what he did want them to think. He wanted them to click him off. He didn't want listeners. He didn't want to do commercials, take requests, play dedications. It wasn't to anyone's ears that he pictured his music traveling when it left the transmitter, but to the deep quiet of the northern night, matching it, reflecting off the stone walls of the abandoned hill farms, the forgotten stands of spruce, the unpeopled hollows to create a harmony so deep and thickly textured that no noise — no hard rock, no blaring commercial, no Weirdness — could ever stain its perfection.

So two sweeps of the second hand to start things off. One hundred and twenty seconds to hide the station in the dark.

It's just past midnight, Saturday February Third. Jupiter is the evening star, the moon is in its waning crescent and two feet of fresh snow lies unblemished on the forest floor. This is A Little Night Music on WKXP, the Voice of the North Country in Verdun, New Hampshire. I'm Terry Silva, and I'll be here straight through until five when Cowboy Bob Adams comes on with the Sunrise Show. Piano music to start things off tonight, followed by some Mahler and then Debussy's La Mer. *If time permits, highlights from Puccini's* Madama Butterfly *with Jussi Bjoerling and Victoria de los Angeles. Music for a snowy night here on KXP.*

And that would be it for the entire five hours. His voice was noise, so he left it out. Listeners were noise, so he refused to admit any. The phone by the console never rang with requests or comments. His only fan letter came after a windy night when the antenna had bucked to even wilder angles than usual, tossing off their signal to a miraculous distance — in this case, to the shores of Hudson Bay. A geologist camped high above the tree line had heard the program on his transistor. He had enjoyed the music, he wrote. The northern lights had been shining in the strange lonely pulsing that can crush a man. In the silence, the music had welled skyward from his tent, filling the night with a beauty that matched the borealis and acted as its support. He was grateful for that. He had only a hazy idea of what the music was and where it came from, but he could tell that whoever was playing it was a good and decent man.

Silva had been proud enough of that letter to leave a

mimeographed copy on Berger's desk. The following night it came back with his response scrawled across the bottom.

"Eskimos don't buy Suburus."

And it was at that moment that Silva decided to go underground. He would not complain about the lack of classical recordings in the station's library. He would say nothing about the thermostat or the miserable pay or Dr. Weird's practical jokes. He would program pieces that were worthy of standing against the utter beauty and simplicity of nothing at all, but other than that he would be silent, the forgotten caretaker of a forgotten space. WKXP, the Mute Voice of the North Country, Radio Nothing.

Beneath his fingers the Beethoven is tugging for its freedom, so he lets it go. Weird often booby-trapped the turntable with bumps manufactured of his snot, but this time the record spins flat and true, filling the studio with sound. Silva waits to coax the needle over the first worn-out groove, then goes out to the lounge in search of untampered coffee. Not finding any, he makes do with nondairy creamer dissolved in hot water.

As usual, he's brought along some papers to grade — an essay on "What I hope to do when I get out of school." As usual, it's a disaster. For one thing, his tenth-graders didn't know what hope meant. And even if they did, there were only two possibilities open: work in the paper mill or cook for tourists. When he had first moved to Verdun he had been a good teacher, perhaps even a brilliant one, but twelve years of being met with the same dull passivity had worn down the edges of his enthusiasm. He looks down at the papers with the grim expression of someone contemplating a clogged-up toilet.

"I think this is an unfair question," the first one begins. Silva reads no further. The second one starts off more promisingly. "I can't wait to graduate and get a good job. Two more years and then freedom, you know Mr. Silva? I've been tossing the idea around and what I would like to do is go to radio school. I think it must be neat, besides what I would really like to do is be wild and stretched out like Dr. Weird. You know, on the limits Mr. Silva? The nite is free cuz the nite belongs to the brave. I say it just like him so I could do it I really could."

At the bottom of the page is an illustration: a skull and crossbones wedged neatly between two horizontal blue lines. Silva stares down at it for a long time, then with a hopeless shrug writes the letter *C* across the top of the page, and then on each remaining paper in the pile.

He's not sure what to do after that. He goes in and checks the teletype, but there's nothing coming in except basketball scores. He reads through Berger's memo on the bulletin board about always making the news upbeat before leading into a commercial. He glances through an article pinned next to it about how Dr. Weird had been voted Broadcaster of the Year in northern New England. He waits until the Beethoven clicks and bumps its way to an end, then — sadly — drops it in the trash with the broken Dvořák. He puts the Mahler cassette on. He goes back into the lounge and tries to concentrate on the Michener novel Sarah had given him for Christmas.

It's about Alaska, which is appropriate enough, but even the steady, simple prose is too much for his concentration. He's restless and not sure why. The storm probably. The wind makes the entire studio throb, right down to the pencils on the desks, and a thin invading edge of snow has begun to creep beneath the outside door. He slides a rug over to dam it, then goes out to the newsroom to empathize some more with the antenna.

He stands there until the Mahler is almost over. It's the *Kindentotenlieder* with Kathleen Ferrier. She sings the last slow lines in the voice that managed like no other to surround tragedy and make it aural, as if what she was drawing upon wasn't breath but the tragic atmosphere of life, letting it course through her throat until only the bittersweet beauty remained. *Sie ruh'n, sie rhu'n wie in der Mutter Haus*, and then the music ends, and he forces himself from his revery, rushing over to the tape machine to switch cassettes.

He's there — he's reaching up to eject the Mahler and insert the Debussy — when there comes a noise so high and piercing it makes him involuntarily double over, as if he has just swallowed the molten Bach once again. Recovering, he immediately checks the dials, expecting to find the antenna had toppled over. But no — the indicators are all fine. He checks the live switch, too, but it's clicked over in the off position. Whatever the sound was, it had to have come from the tape on the air. He pushes the Debussy cassette in, then takes the Mahler over to the extra tape machine and flips on the rewind. He's just begun to play it through again on the cue speakers when the phone rings on the console behind him. It's not loud, more of a liquid gargle than a ring, but since no one had ever called him before, it startles him even more than the screech.

"Hello? Uh, WKXP."

"Are you all right?"

"Sarah? What's wrong?"

"That sound."

"No, listen — is everything okay? Jeff?"

"What was that sound?"

"Something's wrong with the equipment. The Mahler cassette. I was just in the process of checking it out."

"I was sleeping, or at least trying to. The wind's wrenching off the shutters. But then I turned the radio on, and I guess I fell back asleep again and I was dreaming I was at the clinic interviewing a patient, and then there was this sound like a thousand fingernails scratching a blackboard. I never heard anything so terrible."

Sarah's voice was the calm-at-all-costs kind that hinted at more tension than it hid. He tries to picture her lying there in bed, her knees drawn up beneath the silky fabric of her slip, tries to imagine the warmness of the hollow left in the sheets, but it won't come.

"How's Jeff?" he says, as if he hasn't been home in months.

"Restless. He listened to that program tonight after you left. I think it gives him nightmares."

"Dr. Weird? I thought I told you —"

"He sneaks the transistor in the closet where it's dark. What can I do? All his friends listen. They call him a sissy if he doesn't."

"In the closet?"

"It's all part of the ritual. There's a certain way you're supposed to listen. In the dark and alone or something. It's like a club."

Silva feels the blood rush up his head. "You tell him he listens one more time, the radio's going to be trashed."

It seems strange to be talking to her like this. The solitude of the station is so total he feels like a diver at the bottom of a weed-choked sea.

"I hate this weather," she says, filling in his silence. "I think white, I breathe white, I dream white . . . It's endless."

"It's just the usual. I'll shovel in the morning."

"Terry?"

He knows what's coming. He puts his hand up on the earpiece as if to block it.

"Terry, I want to go home."

"This is home."

"You know what I mean. Back to New York."

"With the noise? The muggers? No thanks."

"It's not even different up here anymore. Before we could pretend it was, but it isn't, not in a real sense. Everywhere is the same now. We've been here fifteen years and we still live like strangers. Before we could console ourselves with the forest and the lake and all, but now they've been spoiled, too. If we have to endure ugliness, I want to endure it in a place I belong."

Okay, there it is. The guilt back in place where it belongs — right smack between his eyes. Sarah was still young and beautiful, with a useful, important job, and yet she went around half the time sounding like a solitude-crazed farm wife in Robert Frost. He fingers the tape machine, trying very hard to stay calm.

"Look, Sarah. It's the snow that's bothering you. Things will be clearer in the spring."

"That Weird man. He stopped me today in the supermarket."

"Dr. Weird? What did he do?"

"He winked at me. He licked his lips and patted his stomach. I started to walk around him, then he rattled those razor blades he wears on his ears."

"Did he say anything? . . . Sarah?"

"No."

"Are you sure? What the hell was he even doing there? From what I see of his leavings, the man lives on cocaine and gin."

"He made me feel . . . Oh, I don't know. Strange."

"That's a bright remark."

"Don't start, Terry."

"You already have."

"I'll fall asleep again and that sound will be like a dream or maybe a nightmare. This whole night. I can't tell the difference anymore, that's what scares me . . . Terry, I want to move so bad."

He makes his usual noises of consolation. The spring. Always the spring. After she hangs up, he flicks on the tape machine, trying to locate the sound with more precision. He's too conscientious to leave it hanging like that in midair. He finds the spot where Ferrier's voice diminishes into the last lingering chord, then turns down the gain so as not to be blasted away.

"Okay, screech. You should be right about . . . there."

Even though he's prepared for it this time, the sound still has the capacity to shake him. What's more, it seems to have somehow slipped backward on the tape, totally ruining Ferrier's voice. There's a mechanical quality to the sound that makes him think of the friction of two metals. Iron and lead — something base.

He plays it back three times. By the fourth, the sound seems more focused and intense. It's a few minutes before he realizes that it's coming not only from the Mahler tape, but from the Debussy tape, too — that the two tapes are playing a bizarre duet, one screeching in the studio, one screeching over the air. Along with the shrillness comes a liquid whooshing, as if the metals are being swished rapidly around a porcelain bowl. There's a tremolo in the lower notes that hints of living flesh. Like a cow being chewed apart by a buzz saw — it's the closest analogy he can find.

Whatever, the Debussy is ruined. He shuts it off and

glances up at the clock. Two-thirty. He only has one more record set to play.

This is Terry Silva on KXP, North Country Radio in Verdun, New Hampshire. We've been experiencing technical difficulties, but hopefully they've been rectified. We continue now with highlights from Puccini's Madama Butterfly.

While the love duet is playing, Silva examines the two cassettes with the magnifying glass Weird always left open on his bondage magazines. What he can see of the exposed tape is perfectly smooth. The only thing different are small check marks inked across the corner of the cassettes' labels, as if someone had been crossing them off a list.

Red ink. Red ink the color of blood.

He tears off his earphones and hurries out to the library. The tape cabinet looks normal enough, but when he goes through the cassettes each one has that same check mark there near the composer's name. The Schubert quartets, the Rachmaninoff concertos, the Albéniz. There isn't one Weird had missed.

The memo is attached to the cabinet's side with a magnetic skull-and-crossbones refrigerator ornament the station was giving away in a promotion.

"Yeah, all of them, my-strow. You thought I was fooling? ive jazzed up your act. Stuck in some life. Mood music for the mood im in. Weird sitting in on double screech. You think its ezy playing truth? The nite is strong cuz the nite is brave cuz the nite belongs to moi. Cuz I want your spot, teach. This is the fuckup HamBergers been waiting for. Two hundred bucks of tapes ruined he wont be pleazed. And you dont even love the shit you play enough to fite back thats what gets me. You think the world is all pretty and neat but its now and its nowness and its Weird Weird Weird! Get a vasectomy on your ears, kiche-brain. If HamBerger didnt want to keep the FCC happy youd been out on your ass six years ago. Your too weak to think of getting even so dont even try. im strong and im horny and i take no prisoners. P.S. The next sound you hear destroys test-sickles. Roll over Baytoven, Dr. Weird."

He braces himself for it. He's ready to slap his hands over his ears the moment whatever it is happens. But there's nothing. The Puccini swells over the speakers with its usual surface noise and hesitations, making the lovers seem senile, but other than that, all is fine.

Or temporarily fine. There's only twenty minutes of music on the second side, barely enough time to find something else to play. He can't risk using the cassettes. He goes through the records looking for the least mutilated ones, finally settling on Rubinstein's recording of the Chopin Impromptus. Dr. Weird had taken a bite out of the side, but by lifting the needle over the gap he can get a half hour of play time at least.

A moment after he cues it up on the turntable there is the same screeching noise as before, startling him so much he drops the needle, adding a scratch to Weird's bite. The sound isn't coming over the air this time, but from somewhere inside the studio itself. And the quality is different, too. To the mechanical grinding of the first two sounds is added a distinct element of pain. Not quite human pain, but approaching it. The pain of a robot who has cravings for life.

"Quiet!"

His own vehemence startles him. He can feel himself on the verge of losing control. He closes his eyes to force back the sound, but it only makes it shriller, tightening the intensity until it throbs behind his forehead like a migraine.

"Calmly," he whispers.

The sound rises to a higher pitch. He fights his way in toward Berger's office, bending in half to make progress against the blast. At first, he sees nothing out of the ordinary, then he notices the bottom drawer of Berger's desk is wobbling back and forth as though there's an animal trapped inside. He reaches down to check. There hidden beneath a Dr. Weird souvenir bandanna is a small cassette player rigged to an automatic timer set to go off at 3:00 A.M. sharp.

Silva quickly dismantles it, but the resulting one second of silence is immediately pierced by a louder screech, this one coming from the advertising office. He runs in and dismantles a larger cassette from a larger timer, but then a third screech starts up, then a fourth and a fifth, until finally there is a whole savage choir of screeching cassettes. Joined, the noises take on a scream's throaty vibrato, but it's much worse than any scream. The sound doesn't peak like a scream, doesn't reach a crest and a consequent release. It builds and builds and builds.

Six booby traps go off in all. Silva rushes from one room to the next ripping wires apart like a demolitions expert, sweating from exertion, puffing, his ears shriveling back in self-defense, his throat involuntarily tightening to each new pulse of sound. He finds a seventh booby trap in the freezer compartment of the refrigerator two minutes before it's set to go off. He reaches in to grab it — he starts to pull it out — when there's a snapping noise and a sudden burning pressure on his left thumb.

"Dammit!"

He jerks it back. There affixed to the stub is a mousetrap— the heavy kind with four springs. Yanking if off, he carries cassette player, wires, and clock over to the entrance door, pries it open with his foot, then hurls everything as far out into the snow as he can.

He's panting by the time he's done. His chest heaves up and down — his shirt is wet and sticky against his lower back. He stumbles into the bathroom and splashes cold water against his face, turns toward the toilet, and unzips his pants. He stands there in a daze, not paying attention to what is happening, wanting only to restore the calm balance the sounds have upset. So it isn't until the urine rolls off the toilet onto his shoes that he realizes something is wrong. By the time he understands what, the fluid is flowing across the floor toward the sink.

"Jesus!"

He reaches for some towels. There resting on top of the dispenser is the memo, weighted down by a pretzel-stuffed condom.

"Cellophane over the toilet bowl, thats how pisser. Now look at yourself. A grown man ankle deep in his own filth in Verdun by God New Hampsha. Swim in it, Silva. Your swan song swim. Starting next weekend the nite is mine cuz the nite belongs to those who can keep their p in the pot. All your kulture and brains and where has it got you? im bold and im hungry and i am music and i make them scream. Your wifes not bad, should have seen her looking me over at the Grand Unction. Cute ass like an upside-down heart, tits big hands like mine can just barely cup. Sarah, rite? i can imagine the sounds she makes when shes liking it, how long has that been? Croons, rite? Maybe a nice little moan at the crucifixial moment? ill find out cuz she needs a doctor like me that makes house calls. Your piccolos too tame for her, what the woman wants is a bassoon. She looked at me for a long time and she went to turn away but she couldnt becuz deep inside she knows she needs something wet and wild and wicked and WEIRD. We had a good two minutes eye coitus for openers. P.S. Tell her i liked what she said. Roll over Baytoven, Dr. Weird."

This time Silva doesn't try to straighten things up. He wades right through the middle of the deepest pool, right out through the newsroom, right directly into the library to Weird's three long skull-studded shelves. There's another memo pasted to the top. "You'll never have the nerve," it begins, but he doesn't bother reading the rest. He takes out the first album and places it flat on the uppermost shelf. The Sex Pistols. He takes out the second album and places it flat on top of the first. The Cunning Gulls. He takes out the third album and adds it to the pile. The Straps and Chains. He takes out a fourth album and then a fifth and sixth . . . Sid Vicious, Jesus and the Damned, the Stud Spikes . . . and then the tension and anger inside him become like a spring, and he uses the force of it to take the top record from its sleeve and hurl it with all his strength against the floor.

It hits on edge, compresses, then bounces straight back up again, intact. Furious, he grabs the next record and bends it in half. It folds without cracking, then springs back to shape, intact. He grabs the third record and smashes it as hard as he can over the shelf, but it absorbs the force like a pancake and wobbles to a stop, intact. The fourth record, the fifth and sixth. They bounce away from him like putty.

And with that the spring inside him collapses with a poof that's all but audible. He rubs his stomach. He reaches for the memo that flutters mockingly before his face.

"Anyone with guts would have used an ax. The nite is mine. R. O. B., Dr. Weird."

In the background he can hear the speakers humming their empty electric hum. The Chopin is over. He goes over to the console and stands there watching the turntable spin, without the strength to cue up another record. From off in the distance comes a clicking noise, the kind a cassette makes being rammed home. There's the sound of giggling, then a steadier drone that gradually amplifies itself into recognizable words. It's much softer than the screams, but the gentleness makes it more terrible than anything he has heard so far.

The voice of children chanting in unison.

"We *want* Dr. Weird. We *want* Dr. Weird. We *want* Dr. Weird."

It comes from the speakers in front of him, from the splice machines, from the lounge where he had swallowed the Bach album, from the library with the mutilated tapes. He understands now that there are booby traps set everywhere — that the screams are only the tip of the iceberg; that he can tear them up all night and never get to the end. He sits there with his head braced against his arm as the chanting swells.

"*We want Dr. Weird! We want Dr. Weird. We want Dr. Weird. We want* —"

The chanting stops in mid-phrase, as if the children have been simultaneously throttled by a monster's huge hands. In its place is a silence so deep and tranquil it makes him suspicious, and he feels himself shrinking back in anticipation of the sound that will come next.

The phone. It gargles — stops — gargles again. He reaches for it, but doesn't take it off the receiver. He doesn't want to talk to Sarah, not now. He listens to the sound with a dull kind of dread, wanting to smother it, not knowing how.

Whoever it is refuses to give up. The phone rings so long that he finally convinces himself that it isn't Sarah after all, but someone calling to say how much they miss the music — to ask him where it's gone. He feels a surge of hope. He picks up the phone half expecting to hear the voice of his geologist, calling from the shores of Hudson Bay to tell him the northern lights were pulsing once again.

"WKXP!" he says, with a rush of joy.

There's a hum on the end. Whoever it was has hung up.

Silva puts the phone down and glances up at the studio clock. 4:00 A.M. Slowly, avoiding any sudden movements, he reaches for the Chopin and cues it up again beyond Weird's bite. For a moment the needle hesitates, riding the ridgeline of the battered groove, then with a clicking noise it drops into place.

He plays the Chopin three more times. While it's on he goes around the studio tidying things up as best he can. The broken, mutilated albums he throws in the trash. Dr. Weird's memos he burns. He goes into the bathroom and mops up the urine. He gets the news reports off the teletype and sets it up on the console so Adams can start the morning off easy — he even readies the weather report.

In straightening up the console he finds a record buried beneath some jazz albums sent to them as samples. It's by Tchaikovsky — a new Columbia recording that hasn't even been taken out of its seal. He unwraps it and holds it up to the light, looking for any imperfections or marks. But the record is flawless. It's the only album in the studio Weird had missed.

At precisely 4:45, Adams staggers in the door, his parka cottony with snow. He stamps his feet on the entrance mat and blows melodramatically on his hands. From deep in a pocket he withdraws a Styrofoam cup and waves its steam around in front of him like a censer.

"Hey, Terry boy. Snowing like a son of a bitch, but the roads ain't bad. You listen to the Celtics last night? Bird went bananas. Give me ten minutos, huh?"

He disappears out toward the lounge. Silva reaches forward to shut off the Chopin and flick the live switch into place.

It's four forty-five, Saturday February Third. Venus is the morning star and it glimmers over a white expanse of fresh virgin snow. Good morning. This is Terry Silva here on WKXP, the Voice of the North Country in Verdun, New Hampshire. You've been listening to five hours of A Little Night Music. We'll be back again tomorrow morning with an all-Tchaikovsky program, featuring a new recording of the 1812 Overture with Zubin Mehta and the New York Philharmonic, the United States Military Academy Band, the Cathedral Choir of St. John the Divine, twenty-three howitzers from the Army Museum in Croton-on-Hudson, the bells of St. Thomas Cathedral, and one hundred authentic Brown Bess muskets fired by members of the Reactivated King's Own Dragoons of Wayne County, Pennsylvania. An all-Tchaikovsky festival coming up here on KXP. Until then, this is your host Terry Silva saying . . . Be good.

Adams comes back munching a doughnut. They usually made switching places into an elaborate changing of the guard, complete with salutes and clicking of heels, but this time Silva jerks off the earphones and brushes right past him.

"Hey, what's the matter with you?" Adams yells.

But by then he's already on his way out the door. The first shock of the cold is like a wall, but he dips his shoulder and presses his way through to the car. He starts it up, then goes back outside to work on the windshield. By the time he reaches the road to town, the first light is beginning to seep over the ridge south of the antenna. He stops the car where he always does — on the overlook that takes in the valley in which the town sits.

On a clear morning it was possible to see a third of New Hampshire from there. Hawk Mountain up in Quebec, Ruggles Hump over on the Connecticut, the pulp forest spreading eastward toward Maine, the high summits of the Whites sixty miles south. On a good morning he would take all this in, absorbing the forests and mountains and lakes as if they were a precious form of oxygen necessary to get him through the day.

He gets out of the car and stands there stamping his feet on the overflow from the nearby trash basket. At first, he's afraid the snow will hide the sunrise, but then the flakes scatter apart. Another minute and the sun's leading edge forces itself above the horizon, sending out a fan of red-and-pink ripples. He reaches out his arms as if to cradle the view and lift it bodily into place. He rises up on tiptoes to see farther.

The blue mountains with their smoke of cloud, the sprawling village with its steeples, the white carpet of trees. For a moment they're as perfect as ever, but then the snowflakes rejoin, the wind springs back again, and with a sudden shivering gesture he brings his hands up and clasps them tight over his ears.

yet been developed or spoiled. It was as remote a spot as the Cape had, and yet what he remembered most about it were those things that linked it with all the other places in the country. The beach grass, for instance, that enveloped him when he came back from one of his rowing expeditions; the way the tops intertwined themselves in golden tassels like prairie grass on the Nebraska plains. The way the humid air would be blown out all at once by an exhilarating northwest wind that had more of Colorado in it than Massachusetts. The way the pond was dimpled at dusk by feeding minnows — how the outspreading rings smoothed the water's turbulence and drew the landscape in upon itself, so that by the time the sunset turned purple their cove was as placid and self-contained as a pond on an Indiana farm.

It was the summer he turned twelve — old enough to get serious about two pressing ambitions. The first was to row the family's skiff all the way to Martha's Vineyard and not just the breakwater where the pond opened. The second, more universally, was to see a girl without any clothes on.

Of the two, he spent rather more time working on the first. By August he had gotten his biceps to the point where he could row from the dock to the breakwater in forty minutes flat. He would pause in the channel there at the end of the run, ship oars, and stand precariously upright so he could stare toward the Vineyard, seven miles away — a low smoky shape like a punctured cloud. Beneath him he could feel the incoming tide tugging the skiff back toward home, but at the same time he could feel the horizon tugging him the opposite way, so for that one fragile moment he was equipoised between forces and perfectly content. When the tide became stronger, he brought the stern around and rowed furiously home, working his stroke up to a pitch that nearly burst him, but that would be needed in order to make

any headway against the notorious Vineyard chop. The rest
of the day he would spend going over his equipment list,
reducing to the barest minimum the supplies he could take
along.

These were as follows. Two one-gallon cans of Hawaiian
Punch, to be drunk when necessary, then stowed away beneath the bow seat to serve as sea anchors in case of storm
or water wings in case of swamping. An orange beach umbrella to keep the sun off his neck. A fishing line to use if
the current carried him out to sea and he was starving. A
bottle of ketchup to drown out the fishy taste. Five flash-
lights. A BB gun to use as a deterrent against gulls. Reading
matter in case of boredom — comic books, but also biogra-
phies of Knute Rockne and Jim Thorpe. Matches, their ends
dipped in nail polish. An Esso highway map of southern
New England. Salt tablets. A gallon of antifreeze to pour on
the water in case of sharks.

Fully loaded, the skiff weighed in the neighborhood of 658
pounds. It still wasn't enough, though, and on the day of
the final dress-rehearsal launch his father, in his careful in-
spection, thought of one last thing.

"A compass," he said, frowning in the serious way he had
that lent importance to all of Peter's projects. "What happens if it's foggy out and you miss the Vineyard? The next
stop after that is Brazil."

They went out and bought a compass that same morning,
but it still put a damper on things. There were a lot of foggy
days in August, and Peter didn't like the thought of rowing
all by himself to Brazil. More and more his thoughts began
trending toward the fulfillment of his second summertime
ambition: to sneak through the pitch-pine woods that began
past their driveway, then the cranberry bog beyond that,
then the fence beyond that until he reached the high, con-

cealing meadow grass surrounding the bunkhouses of Camp Merry B. Wampanoag for Girls.

He had no idea what he would do once he got there. See a naked girl, he supposed. But what that meant he wasn't sure, no more than he was sure what would happen when he finally took the skiff out into the choppy waters of Vineyard Sound. At night after everyone had gone to bed, he would lower himself feet first through his window outside, crawling past the cars and the drying beach towels until he reached the protection of the first brittle pines.

But once gained, the woods only confused him. The dark marbled shadows from the moonlight became mixed with the dark marbled thoughts in his head until he all but reeled from excitement and skipped toward the cranberry bog like a horny chipmunk. By the time he reached the bog he was completely disoriented; he tried wading across, but the mud was too thick for him; he tried circling around one side, but the bog was endless. In the end he would find the highest rise he could and stand there blinking his flashlight toward the unreachable camp, hoping by some miracle the beams would find a magic current and become X rays powerful enough to penetrate bunkhouse walls.

They never did. After a while the batteries would start to wear down, and he would have to find his way home in the dark, chilled now from bog water, his pants ripped from thorns. When he came back from his rowing trips he always felt cleansed and uplifted, but these nighttime crawls left him feeling humiliated, defeated past words. He would karate chop any tree that got in his way, kick the thinner ones, scream at the top of his lungs so as not to be crushed from sheer implosion of the groin.

The last of these trips — the one he went on the night

before the Gerards came — was particularly disastrous. He lost the flashlight in the bog, karate chopped a sapling that turned out to be an iron boundary post, and fell into one of the pit traps his younger brother, Gordon, was always setting for raccoons. By the time he returned to the driveway he was beaten and in tears. His father's voice, gentle as it was, fell across his back like the last stroke of the lash.

"That you, Peter?"

He was standing in the circle of cedar where the flagpole was, dressed in the gym shorts that were all he ever wore to bed, his shoulders as white and full as a sail.

"Yeah, Pop. It's me."

Peter stepped into the circle ready to raise his hands like a prisoner turning himself in. His father, seeing the scratches on his face, the tatters on his shirt, only smiled.

"Been out for a stroll, have you?"

Peter thought fast. "I was out checking the oyster traps."

He wasn't sure why he said it. There were no oyster traps in the pond, not even any oysters, but it was the first thing that came to mind. His father nodded at this in his grave, thoughtful way. Peter could have told him he'd just gotten back from Uranus and he would have nodded. Perhaps because his own life had been filled with so many disappointments, he was the kind of man who understood the correct proportions of dreams.

"I couldn't sleep myself," he said, gesturing vaguely toward the house. "I've been awake violating one of our rules. I was listening to the news."

There was an actual list with these rules, pasted to the refrigerator door where guests couldn't miss it. The first rule was about not mixing burnables with nonburnables in the trash; the last rule forbade academic gossip at the dinner table or in the boats. Not listening to the news was some-where toward the middle of the list, just before the one about not complaining about the rain.

"You listened to the news?" Peter said, putting all the ac-cusation in his tone he could.

"Yep. The entire five minutes. I listened out on the porch where your mother couldn't hear. I've been doing it all sum-mer."

Strange as his confession was, what he did next was even stranger. He crossed over to the flagpole and started unfas-tening the rope from its metal cleat.

This flagpole was the highest on the pond, a proud var-nished thing of genuine beauty. His father had carved it himself from a white pine that had come crashing down on the roof during Hurricane Carol back in the Fifties; the flag that flew there was the old kind with forty-eight stars, and they kept it flying night and day in defiance of all conven-tion.

It only took a moment to loosen the rope. The pulley on top made a squeaky sound, then warbled like a bird. His father, staring upward, lowered the flag until it was halfway down the pole, tied the rope back around the cleat, then — after hesitating — added two knots more.

"There," he said. "I think we'll leave it like that for a while." He rubbed his hands on his shorts like a man who has just finished a heavy piece of work, and put one of them on Peter's shoulder. "All set now, son? We'd better get some sleep in. We'll need all our energy for the Gerards."

Peter's first thought when he woke up in the morning was that the entire episode had been a dream. But no — when he rushed outside to check there was the flag at half-mast where his father had put it. It didn't look airy and perky like it usually did. The fabric, wet from ground mist, clung list-lessly to the pole.

In a way he couldn't understand, the lowered flag seemed to set the mood for the entire day. Over the pond the fog was heavy and lifeless, pressed down by heat. The crickets back in the meadow sounded labored and slurred. Socrates, their Labrador, had already dug a hole for himself in the cool dirt behind the bulkhead. It was going to be hot, brutally hot. His father was rigging a tarpaulin over the patio to keep off the sun. His mother, her face dabbed in mayonnaise, was mixing chicken salad in the deep green bowl she only used when they had guests.

There were a lot of these each summer. His father liked to have the younger faculty members down; his mother was always inviting her French majors, so there were few days when the lawn and beach weren't noisy with happy sounds. Most of these guests were in their twenties, athletic and handsome. They would overcrowd the sailboat and laugh when it capsized; there were furious games of water polo that churned the water into froth. And while Peter still thought of his future as something distant, something that had to be rowed to or snuck up on and only achieved with tremendous effort, they were on the very edge of their destinies and bright with it — bright and sunny and wet.

The Gerards were in a different category altogether. What this category was, it was difficult to say. "Our distant rela-tions," his father said, and left it at that. "Those poor people in the truck," was how Gordon put it, snobby at seven. "A good Catholic family from Providence," said his mother, shaking her head in a way that managed to combine nine parts admiration with one part distaste.

It was this last phrase that summed them up best. The Gerards were Baptists, not Catholics, but there was a generosity about them both in number and in spirit that was reminiscent of the huge, fiercely loyal Italian families in the North End. Aunt Alice had already given birth to four kids by then, and there would be another three before she was through. She had a bosom as wide as Kate Smith's, a laugh so deep it could make your ribs rattle, and a total disregard for what you did or where you were from or anything except whether or not you were the kind of person who could look life in the face without flinching.

Uncle Norbett, perhaps because he worked bottling Coke all day, was much quieter — the kind of man who liked to wear green work clothes even on his days off. As a boy, he had worked as a logger in Maine and knew the names of every tree just by examining the bark. He was always chiding his wife about something or other, acting as the gentle brake on all her enthusiasms; "Now Alice" was his favorite phrase. The two of them were always holding hands with each other or with one or more of their kids. The Gerards were the kind of family that even then was almost extinct — the kind that presented themselves to the world not as separate individuals but as one unseverable chain.

They arrived at eleven, just as the heat became unbearable. Socrates heard them first — he barked once for form's sake, then ran off to hide in the garden. A moment later their horn could be heard as they pulled off the macadam onto the dirt, and a moment after that, Gordon, posted as lookout, came tearing down the driveway pursued by a vast cloud of dust.

"They're here!" he yelled, though it was hardly necessary. "Mom! Pop! They're here!"

The horn beeped louder, there was the sputtery clanking

noise of bad gears being thrown into neutral, and then around the driveway's last curve in a shimmer of heat waves coasted the Gerard's orange van.

Their arrival was always the same. Before the doors were opened, before the van had even stopped, the kids were squirming backward through the windows, so there was a good fifty yards between the spot where the first one landed and where the last one tumbled out. They immediately gathered themselves into a swarm and set out for the beach, not to be seen again until lunchtime. Norbett, waving his porkpie hat, jumped out the driver's seat and trotted around to help Alice down. She had remarkable daintiness for a woman her size, and held her hand out to him with all the dignity of a Fijian queen. Once established on the ground, she immediately swung her arms open, ready to embrace the first thing that came into reach.

It was Gordon this time — at the sight of her smile, all his snobbiness melted away. A moment later Peter's father was there, then his mother, and there were kisses all around and handshakes and the quick unpacking of hampers, coolers, and kegs.

"We've brought some hamburg," Alice said, holding out a basketball-sized wad of wax paper. "Throw it right into the chicken salad, Barbara — Norbett likes his substance. Here's some watermelon to go into the icebox. David, you're handsomer and more distinguished every year. That beard suits you. Where's that pooch gone off to, I've brought a bone. Socrates! Now don't say anything but I've baked some pies and later we'll go out and get ice cream to put on top. Wipe that smile off your face, Peter. Haven't you ever seen a fat woman perspire? Now get busy and help your uncle unload those chairs."

It was because there was no refusing one of Alice's commands — because he stood toward the back of the van, reaching in to pull out the last supplies — that Peter turned out to be the one to see them first. But even Peter, quick as he was, didn't see them actually descend. They were just there — there like people on a police lineup or a slave platform are there, without any preliminaries.

They held hands and faced him, smiling bashfully. The girl was about nineteen, pretty in an average sort of way, with blonde hair piled over her head like a swirl of banana ice cream. She had on a white blouse that was feminine and soft-looking; below it was a miniskirt that showed off two crusty, angry red knees. Seeing Peter stare, she dropped her eyes to the ground, tucked her head into her shoulder, and began very carefully to scratch.

The man was about the same age. Like her, he was the kind of person your eyes could slip right off without seeing. He had acne. He had red hair cut short in bristles. His complexion, like hers, was unhealthily pale — the white of the generic cartons that were just then starting to show up on the supermarket shelves.

So it wasn't anything about his looks that captured Peter's attention, it was what he was wearing. Not the Levi's that might be expected, not the shorts or bell-bottomed cords. This average-looking man of average height and average weight and average probably intelligence had on baggy green army fatigues that — after billowing out around his waist like bloomers — bunched in tight to his calves and disappeared into the blackest, shiniest, hottest-looking combat boots Peter had ever seen.

Seeing their polish was like watching a light flash on. It was the only thing about either of them that possessed any vibrancy or life.

"Hey," the man said, with a trace of a drawl. He looked down at his hand to see if it was dirty, rubbed it vigorously on his belt, then stuck it out in Peter's direction. "Danny Doe like in John?" He tilted his head the barest minimum. "The wife."

The girl was looking up at the trees like someone seeing skyscrapers for the first time. Realizing she'd been introduced, she stuck her hand out, too, and opened her mouth just far enough for Peter to see she was chewing purple gum.

"Hi ya," she said.

Around on the other side of the van things were finally sorting themselves out. Aunt Alice, who liked billowy dresses and always seemed a step ahead of her own blur, came over to formally introduce everyone. Peter wasn't sure, but there seemed to be something hesitant in the way she did this; finishing, she stood back and watched them like a matchmaker anxious everyone should get along.

"These are the Does," she explained. "Doreen is Gouger Rogowski's cousin twice removed. You remember Gouger, don't you, David? That makes her my third cousin, if that still counts. She lives in Cranston, or at least she's going to now. And this," she said, worry creeping into her tone, "is Danny Doe. Danny's a private in the Army, from South Carolina originally, right, Danny? He's on leave so we can't stay very long. Danny and Doreen, I want you to meet our other cousins, the Shrivers."

The Does smiled, passively, and moved a step closer together.

"It's all right we brought them along, isn't it, Barbara?" Alice asked. "I would have called, but it all came about very suddenly."

"Of course, of course," Peter's mother said, frowning the

way she did whenever she was computing portions. "Uh, would they care to go for a swim before lunch?"

Danny mumbled something in Alice's direction. "They don't swim," Alice said.

"Oh. Well, would they care to lie out in the sun then?"

Danny mumbled something again. "She burns," Alice said.

"Oh," Peter's mother said. "She burns."

Everyone would have stood there forever if it wasn't for Peter's father. He waved his arm around in a gesture that took in everything and made his voice turn hearty.

"Well that's fine then and you two make yourselves right at home. We have the hammock all rigged up. There are plenty of beach chairs around. Peter will lend you his fishing rod if you don't mind catching snappers. We're glad you're here and if there's anything you want just give a yell."

His father was hard to resist when he spoke that way. The Does walked slowly in the direction of the water, as if his hand were on their backs pushing. By the time they got to the stairs leading to the beach they had stopped again. They stood there holding hands looking down to where the Gerard kids splashed in their floats.

Under normal circumstances Peter would have been down there with them, showing off his skiff. But so unexpected was the Does' appearance there, so out of character Alice's worried tone, that he lingered behind hoping to get some more information.

It was Alice who explained things, talking quickly in case they came back. The Does had only been married eight weeks, she said, Doreen having met him when she had gone down to Georgia to visit her brother Mark in basic training. They had lived for a while on base, but with Danny due to

be shipped out any moment, she had moved back to Cranston to her folks'.

It was the next part of the story that was extraordinary,
at least to Peter. Danny, having just graduated from ad-
vanced infantry school in Oklahoma, was in the middle of a
twenty-four-hour pass that had started twelve hours ago
back in Fort Sill. By hopping a transport to Chicago, then a
regular shuttle flight to Boston, then a Trailways bus, he had
managed to reach Cranston at ten that morning in time to
surprise Doreen just as she was climbing into the Gerard's
van for the drive to Cape Cod — a drive that was originally
intended to cheer Doreen up. There was a transport back to
Oklahoma leaving Otis Air Force Base at four o'clock in the
afternoon. Danny would have to be on it or risk going
AWOL.

Two things about this story mystified Peter. The first was
that a man would travel four thousand miles to spend six
hours with a girl like Doreen. The second concerned the
word Alice had used when she told them where he was being
shipped out to. She had said it quickly the way his mother
did whenever she lapsed into French — quickly, in a blur of
unintelligible syllables that left Peter groping. Where? he
wanted to say, but Alice was already past it onto something
else.

"There's no bus to Otis, is there? We'll drive him then.
Doreen was so surprised to see him I thought she'd faint.
Time for lunch and a swim and we'll be going. But it's good
they got together even for a little while." She hesitated —
her face, usually so vibrant, was as limp and heavy as the
flag. "Things being what they are, that is."

No one said anything when she finished; everyone turned
to stare toward the cove. Instead of going down to the beach,

the Does had walked toward the trees that began there on the cliff's edge. They were scrub oak and maple mostly — green and inviting from the distance, but littered with poison sumac and thorns. The Does started in anyway; Danny pushed one of the branches out of their way, then quickly drew back his hand, stung. They both took a step backward with that. They stood peering into the shrubbery like children on the marge of an impenetrable jungle.

"What time is it?" Peter's mother asked.

Uncle Norbett squinted down at his watch. "Eleven thirty-five."

"They're welcome to use the boats," Peter's father said. He cupped his hands around his mouth. "You're welcome to use the boats!"

The Does remained where they were, staring into the woods. Alice, without losing her worried expression, forced out a laugh.

"Here we are standing out in the hot sun like somebody's concrete statuary. David, I want to inspect your garden. Our eggplant is mushy this year. Peter, you go down and see my babies don't drown. Norbett, there's your hammock sitting ready for use. Say what you want to, there's no place like the Cape on a nice summer day."

For a while after that things were normal. His mother busied herself getting lunch ready, Alice went around inspecting his father's latest improvements, and Norbett fell asleep beneath the apple tree just as he did every year. For a while it was easy to pretend there was nothing different about this visit than any of the visits that had come before, but then Peter would look up and see the Does standing by themselves on the lawn holding hands and feel a strange prickly sensation on the back of his head that left him feeling irritated and confused.

There was an old Wilson football lying abandoned in the grass. Danny, after staring down at it for five minutes, picked it up and threw it in a clumsy spiral toward the bird feeder. When it landed, he went over and threw it back toward the clothesline. Doreen walked with him between throws. Except for this and going over to stare into the trees once and a while, they did nothing else until lunchtime.

They ate on the patio beneath the tarpaulin his father had rigged for the sun. As shady as it was, the air was lifeless and it was an effort just to pass around the various dishes. The Does ate with the same shy, slow motion in which they did everything else. Peter, sitting across from them, watched in fascination as they poured ketchup over their cole slaw and stirred with their forks until everything was red.

"Can I ask you something?" Danny said, leaning over. He lowered his voice and clamped one eye shut in a wink. "There any snakes in those woods back there?"

Certain questions startle a lie out of you. "Yes," Peter said, though there weren't.

Danny's frown, already droopy, sagged even further. "Told ya!" Doreen said triumphantly, but her expression was crestfallen, too, and after a few listless tries they put their forks down and sat there like kids waiting patiently to be excused.

Up the table, the others were already finishing. The ice cream was brought out, served, then gulped down before melting; Norbett took a carving knife and sliced apart the watermelon in a dozen quick whacks. Lunch with the Gerards was usually a noisy, drawn-out affair lasting half the afternoon, and here they were pushing back their chairs ten minutes after they'd sat down.

"Everyone's acting nuts today," Peter mumbled.

No one heard him. On the edge of the patio was a redwood chair with an umbrella mounted on the back. Danny stood beside it saying something to Alice, who looked off toward the water and bit her lip. Not right then, but a few minutes later she came over to where Peter's mother was wiping off the picnic table with a wet paper towel.

"May I ask a favor, Barbara?" she said, in an oddly formal tone. "Danny and Doreen are a bit tired out after all the excitement. They wanted to know if it was all right for them to take a nap somewhere."

"A nap?" His mother's eyes met Alice's and something was exchanged there too quickly for Peter to tell what. "There's Peter's room. They can have that, I suppose. We haven't gotten around to insulating the ceiling yet. This time of day it's hotter than an oven."

"Oh, that's okay," Alice said. "They just want to take a nap, just a short one."

The conversation was normal enough, but both women seemed relieved when it was over. Alice went back and said something to Danny; Danny turned and said something to Doreen. A moment later they disappeared through the screen door into the house, holding hands with each other but differently than before, tighter somehow, higher.

"Just a little nap," Alice whispered, watching them trudge off. "We'll give them an hour, then it will be time to go. . . . Hey!" she yelled, as if the thought had just struck her. "I don't know about you two, but I'm dying for a swim."

A swim for Aunt Alice meant wading around the shallows with her dress bunched up around her waist. But at least it got everyone moving again. The water felt like hot alphabet soup, one of the Gerard kids thought he saw a jellyfish and Gordon cut his foot on a shell, but for an hour or more they all went through the motions of a good time.

It was the heat that ended things. Once the sun got above the cliff it was unbearable, and one by one they all began drifting back to the patio and its shade. The kids spread their beach towels out on the cold stone and fell asleep immediately; the adults lay back in their lounge chairs, fanned themselves with paper plates, and made a labored attempt at conversation.

"Do you remember Johnny Potter?" Alice asked. "Johnny Potter. Al Prince's nephew."

His father folded his plate over his nose. "No."

"I saw him the other day. He's aged."

Norbett nodded his head up and down. "It's tough going overseas. I remember the time I went. It was on the *Queen Mary* in January of '43 and it was the coldest morning in the history of the world."

It seemed like the start of a story, but he didn't tell one. "It's tough going overseas," he said.

"Overseas." His father made a tasting motion with his lips. "It's a funny word."

"Overseas," his mother said. "It makes you think of movement and spray."

They passed the word around their circle like a tray of cool drinks. For a time they were able to talk about other things, able to keep their eyes on something besides the corner of the house where Peter's bedroom was. But like a magnet, it kept drawing them back.

"A man's got to serve," Norbett said, talking louder but without conviction. "Say what you want to, a man's got to serve."

"That ridiculous cowboy," his father said. "All this talk about dominoes. I believe despite all his advisers he must be a stupid, cowardly man."

"What time is it?" Alice mumbled, as if she didn't want to know.

"Isn't right," Norbett said. "Isn't right at all."

What wasn't right? Dominoes weren't right? Cowboys weren't right? What did they mean? Peter wondered. They said it to nobody, just said it to thin air, and turned to stare with helpless expressions toward the corner where Doreen and Danny had gone for their nap. Even later, when they lay their heads back against the cushions and added their snoring to the abrupter breathing of the kids, it wasn't as if they had really gone to sleep but were pretending to, closing their eyes out of sheer modesty and not fatigue.

Peter himself closed his eyes, as if to experience what they felt, but there was nothing there for him except heat and white flashes and a grainy kind of buzz. It was too hot to go to sleep — his chest raced with too many hard things. Anger that he hadn't been consulted about giving up his room, embarrassment to think of the Does opening his closet and finding his stuffed animals, fear they would get clumsy and disrupt his collection of shells. These things, and then something vaster than these, an intense curiosity that was similar to what he felt when he thought about reaching new water in his skiff — like this and like the more tormenting curiosity he felt when he began his nightly trips toward the cranberry bog and the unreachable girls' camp on the far side.

He looked around the patio to make sure everyone was still asleep. Slowly, not making any sound that would give him away, he got up from the chair, tiptoed over to the edge of the patio, and let himself down onto the grass. His mother's hydrangea began there, and in a flash he was down on his knees behind the first of them, scuttling toward the house with the light agility of a crab.

The ground by the foundation was packed dirt, cool and mossy. He took a left at the first corner, peeked cautiously around the second, then made a left around that one, too. There was an exposed section where he had to crawl out around the bulkhead, but once past it the roses began and he was able to slither through the space left between the thorns and the foundation with inches to spare.

His room had two windows on that side. The first was too high, so he kept crawling until he reached the second. He pressed his ear to the siding, hoping to hear something, but there was nothing besides the same vacant rush he got whenever he put his ear to a shell. Slowly now, scarcely breathing, he rearranged himself on his knees and began boosting himself up inch by inch until his head reached the level of the window and he was able to see in.

He wasn't sure how long he stayed there. Thirty seconds. A minute. When he had seen all there was to see, he let himself back down, retraced his route through the roses, and emerged on the open lawn on the patio's far side.

He had done all this coolly and very calmly, like a professional spy. The minute he hit the lawn, though, the accumulated tension became too much for him and he popped to his feet like an unwound spring. Throwing off his shirt, he raced down the stairs to the dock, hurled himself into the skiff, pulled at the painter until it came loose, rammed the oars into the oarlocks, and began rowing furiously toward the breakwater, starting out at a pace that was twice as fast as any he had ever managed, then increasing it past that into something phenomenal. When he reached the breakwater he pulled hard on the starboard oar and skidded the boat around again toward home, his eyes blinded from sweat running down his forehead, his heart seared from pumping, his mind a mad tumbling torment of all he had seen.

The Gerards were leaving when he got back. Norbett had succeeded in wedging all the kids into the van — they draped themselves out the windows and made frantic grasping motions, as if to hold the afternoon back. Alice sat in the front seat with the happiest expression she had worn all day. She put her face to the windshield and blew kisses as Norbett backed up.

"Take Davisville up to Isaac Perkins Road, then cut over on that!" his father yelled. "It'll bring you out to Otis in plenty of time."

Danny and Doreen were the last ones to get in. There was no change in their expression, no alteration in the shy impassivity they had hid in ever since they had arrived. Doreen's makeup had turned syrupy in the heat; a few strands of hair had tumbled loose from her bouffant. It almost made her look pretty, but she didn't know it and pushed the curl back.

Danny held his hand out to help her into the van, then turned around and wiped the other hand against his fatigues and stuck it out in his father's direction.

"Thank you for having us, sir," he said in his soft drawl. He looked around, taking in the house, the garden, and the cove as if only now really seeing them. "Nice place." He shook his head slowly from side to side. "Real nice place."

"Good-bye!" Alice yelled. "See you next year, everyone!"

Norbett goosed the motor, Danny spun around and with a grace Peter wouldn't have credited him with, boosted himself into the accelerating van and slid shut the door.

"See you next year!" yelled Gordon, running after them. "See you next year!" yelled his father and mother. "See you next year!" Peter yelled, the words making no sense to him, his throat swollen tight.

They could hear the horn beeping all the way up the driveway, then all the way up the dirt road onto the macadam, until finally the sound grew fainter and became mixed with the lighter, happier sound of distant laughter and tinkling glasses that always seems to well up with the haze of a Cape Cod afternoon.

"Well," his mother said. "That's that."

She said it every year, but it sounded different this time. His father, who missed nothing, was ready with a surprise.

"Let's drive to Woods Hole and get some steamers," he said. "Gordon, you go lock up Socrates. It's too hot to stay home. Besides . . ." He shrugged. "It's been a long day."

"I'm not going," Peter said.

His parents looked at him. "Peter," his mother began, but something in his expression made her stop. "There's chicken salad left in the refrigerator. You can heat up some rolls if you want. We won't be gone long."

It was hazy until sunset, then it rained hard for half an hour, the drops sizzling off everything they hit. Peter, exhausted from rowing, shy of his bedroom, fell asleep on the living room couch and didn't wake up until he heard the car door slam out by the garden.

"Shhh, don't wake him," his father whispered.

He fell asleep again after that, and when he woke up it was midnight and much cooler. He groped around the closet until he found his father's sweater, then stumbled outdoors onto the lawn. He was in the dreamy, lazy state that follows hard upon exhaustion when things that happened a few hours ago already seem inconceivably remote. Had the Gerards really come? There were empty soda cans on the patio, their lids silvery and wet, but it was the only evidence he found.

Peter walked toward the water with no fixed intention.

The moon was full, and it would have been a perfect night to crawl to Camp Wampanoag, but for some reason the fierce desire he usually felt wasn't there. Instead, he continued down the steps and balanced his way out the dock to its end.

The pond was still after the rain. The moon was low enough that its beams came diagonally across the surface of the water, casting a narrow band of milkiness from the far shore to his feet. As he stood there watching it, looking for the chop in the surface that meant feeding blues, something remarkable happened. A swan, one of six the pond was home to, swam across the farthest, broadest part of the band, its head upright and curious, its wings puffed and feathery, its motion stately without strain. Peter stared at it as he had never stared at anything before, trying to make the seeing so hard and so permanent it would never leave him. He knew, without anyone telling him, it was the most beautiful sight he had ever seen.

It didn't last long. By the time he really saw it the swan was past the band into the darkness. As it disappeared — in the regret of the moment's passing — he felt a chill settle across his shoulders and his intuition take a sudden leap ahead. All summer long his knowing had butted itself against the secret, unreadable blankness of things, and now suddenly here it was past them, skipping ahead the way a twelve-year-old's imagination sometimes will, so that the truths that come then are often the most lasting. He knew, watching the swan glide off, that whatever else happened in the future, life would continue to present itself to him in that same shimmery, ungraspable way — that behind distant islands and distant girls' camps and lowered flags and adult silences was nothing he could isolate and give answers to, nothing concrete, but only these intertwined bewildering strands of beauty and sadness and mystery combined.

Doreen, that is, on her knees by the side of the bed, her hair stroked by a Danny who is crying. Doreen on her knees resting her cheek against the side of Danny's leg, crying likewise. Doreen with her chewing gum reaching down to tie with inexpressible tenderness the laces of her husband's boots.